# DEADPOINT

orca sports

# DEADPOINT

## NIKKI TATE

ORCA BOOK PUBLISHERS

**Library and Archives Canada Cataloguing in Publication**

Tate, Nikki, 1962–, author
Deadpoint / Nikki Tate.
(Orca sports)

Issued in print and electronic formats.
ISBN 978-1-4598-1352-6 (paperback).—ISBN 978-1-4598-1353-3 (pdf).—
ISBN 978-1-4598-1354-0 (epub)

I. Title. II. Series: Orca sports
PS8589.A8735D43 2017     jc813'.54     C2016-904457-2
C2016-904458-0

First published in the United States, 2016
Library of Congress Control Number: 2016949044

**Summary:** In this high-interest sports novel, Ayla must face her fears and make
her way back down the mountain after a guide is injured in a climbing accident.

*Orca Book Publishers is dedicated to preserving the environment and has printed
this book on Forest Stewardship Council® certified paper.*

Orca Book Publishers gratefully acknowledges the support for its publishing
programs provided by the following agencies: the Government of Canada
through the Canada Book Fund and the Canada Council for the Arts,
and the Province of British Columbia through the BC Arts Council
and the Book Publishing Tax Credit.

Cover photography by Nikki Tate
Author photo by Ana Vodusek

ORCA BOOK PUBLISHERS
www.orcabook.com

Printed and bound in Canada.

20   19   18   17   •   4   3   2   1

*For Allegra—with fond memories of climbs we've done together in the past and looking forward to more adventures in the future.*

# Chapter One

Take any climbing accident where someone gets badly hurt or dies. Try to figure out what went wrong. Say at the climbing gym a climber falls from near the top of the wall. Nosebleed territory. Two broken ankles, bruised ribs, maybe a concussion. Maybe passed out cold. Maybe, on a really bad day, dead. Dead. Dead.

"Ayla! Just go for it. My neck is killing me!"

Lissy, my belay partner, is three stories below me. She takes up the slack in the rope as I climb. Even though the music is blaring through the gym speakers, I can hear her just fine. But nothing blocks out the voice in my head, the one that always starts nagging as I get near the top of the wall. *Seven things,* the voice reminds me. *In a bad accident, an average of seven things will go wrong. Are you ready to die?*

I lean back, away from the wall, my arms straight to help save what little strength I have left.

"You can do this!" Lissy shouts up to me.

What I should be thinking about is where to put my feet. Which of the small blue knobby holds will give me the best route to the top. Instead, I look down at the knot snug at the front of my climbing harness. This is my end of the same rope that loops up to the top of the wall and back down to Lissy. If that knot slips, if the rope snaps, if Lissy gets distracted and lets go...if I fall. But any one of those things is not likely to happen alone. That's the point of the seven-factors-behind-every-disaster theory.

Both Lissy and I would have to forget to double-check the knot. Something weird would have to happen to distract Lissy. One of the gazillion boys Lissy likes would have to phone her *and* her phone would have to be turned on with the ringer loud enough for her to hear. At the same time, the music in the gym would have to be so loud that I wouldn't notice she was being distracted. Maybe there were already seven factors I didn't even know about all lined up. Maybe I was about to plummet backward toward the ground with no hope of surviving.

"Come on, Ayla! Christmas is coming!"

I let go with my left hand and reach around behind me to dip into my chalk bag. Sweaty fingers won't help with the final few moves. Maybe sweaty fingers is factor number seven. I'll slip off the hold, take an awkward fall, and distracted Lissy will be caught off guard at the same moment she stops to unkink her neck.

*Just go.* This isn't about speed. Not tonight. It's about getting it right.

Climbing well. My left leg is quivering, and climbing well is feeling less and less important as each breath I suck in gets more panicky.

There's a hold by my left knee. I can get there with my left foot. Done. Then a smooth reach up to the decent shell-shaped grip above my right hand. Shift my weight off my right foot so it can move off to the side. Yes. Brace against the wall. No hold there, but balance, balance.

"Good! You've got this, no problem!"

I make the mistake of glancing down at Lissy's upturned face so far below me.

"Don't," I whisper, turning my head back to focus on the anchor just above. Two more moves and I will be there.

I am balanced and held securely by the rope tied with that perfect knot at the front of my harness. It *is* perfect, isn't it? I *did* check, didn't I? My breathing is faster now, rough and shallow. My tongue presses against the roof of my mouth. Everything is dry, dry, dry. Am I hydrated enough? What if

I lose consciousness? Can't that happen if you get dehydrated? What if I slip? Let go?

"Breathe, you idiot. You've done this before." Even though there's nobody else on the routes to either side of me, I barely move my lips as I whisper to myself.

"Come on, Ayla. You can do this! My mom is waiting outside!"

I close my eyes and try to swallow, except there is nothing to swallow.

"Ayla! There's a good hold for your left foot just over to the side. See it?"

Near the top of the wall is the worst place to get stuck. Up here nothing makes sense. Up here my reptile brain is screaming at me that the rope will snap, the anchor will break free, my belayer's mother will charge into the gym and make her drop the rope. I will fall, and I will die. Or wind up in a body so broken I will spend the next fifty years wishing I had died. And when my brain starts to think like this, there is no logic. It's not like I can just pull myself together. It doesn't matter that the knot on my harness is as secure as it was when I started up the wall. Or that my belayer has never let me down. It doesn't even matter that I have climbed this wall before.

My heart turns over in the tight space inside my chest. Most climbing accidents happen at the end of a session. People push too hard. They are tired. That's when mistakes get made.

The little brass bell at the top of the wall, the one I should be able to get to and ring, is so close. I can see the tiny clapper, the delicate chain suspending the bell from a hook right at the top. I won't be ringing it tonight.

"Take!" I call down.

"Need a rest?" Lissy asks as she takes the slack out of the rope. I feel a comforting tug at my waist as she holds me safe.

"Lower," I answer.

"But you're almost there! Two more moves!"

"I'm done." I lean back into the harness, push my feet against the wall and let go of the hold. "Bring me down."

I can imagine Lissy's thoughts as she begins to lower me and the ground inches closer. She's thinking I will never be a great climber, that she is wasting her time coming to the gym with me. She's thinking I should take up another sport. Something easier. Something safer. Soccer maybe. Or golf.

My feet touch down beside her and she grins. "Good fight," she says. "Next time. You'll nail it next time."

Standing beside her, safe on the ground, her words seem reasonable. "Thanks." But what I'm thinking is that it's getting harder and harder to find reasons to come to the gym. Would our friendship survive if one day I walked out of the gym and never came back?

## Chapter Two

Lissy is so close behind me I can hear her breathing. Neither of us says anything. We don't have to. The new boy on the wall has our full attention. He is so good. It's like he has glue pads on his fingers or suction cups on the bottom of his climbing shoes. He's like one of those cute frogs from the Amazon with the blobby toes. Or a gecko. Or a fly. Normally I would say something encouraging, but there's no need. He is handling the bouldering route we call

Turtle Alley like he's strolling down a sidewalk. Effortless. Smooth.

I've never made it to the top of Turtle Alley. There's a move around an overhang that has me beat. The hold on the other side is just out of reach. My fingers have grazed it, but I've never been able to grab on. This boy, though. He takes a deep breath, moves his left foot to a tiny nub of a hold under the overhang. It's more like a pimple than a hold. But it's just enough that when he pushes hard with his other foot and takes a big swing with his left hand and then immediately his right, he's able to grab onto the elusive hold. He must have incredible abs, because he's holding his hips in close as he moves his left foot up around the corner. He hooks his heel on a small block and then pulls himself up and around in one smooth motion. I hardly know where to look. Everything is moving—not fast but all connected, balanced. And then he's at the top of the bouldering problem, both hands securely on the last hold. It's a juggy thing that looks like a turtle's back. He glances behind him, and Lissy and I take half a step back to get out of his way as he drops back down to the mats.

"I'm Carlos," he says with a quick grin. "That was fun. Overhang was kind of a challenge."

"It took me a week to get that one," Lissy says.

I can't stop gawking at this new Carlos boy, who leaves a smear of chalk over his eyebrow when he pushes his straight, black hair out of his eyes.

"I'm Lissy—and this is my friend Ayla," Lissy says, elbowing me in the side.

"Hi," I manage to choke out.

"You guys just get here?" Carlos asks as if he's the one on home turf.

Lissy nods. "Want to warm up with bouldering?" she asks me, even though we had planned to start on an easy roped climb on the big wall. "What about right here?"

Carlos grins. "I'll watch, maybe get some tips." He flops down on the mat beside my feet. I guess we're staying. Lissy dips her fingertips into her chalk bag and blows off the excess.

"Have fun," I say and step off to the side. No way I'm starting with Turtle Alley. Definitely not in front of Carlos. I pick something easier close by and turn to face the wall. Colored tape marks the start of the short route. We don't need ropes in this part of the gym. The climbs are never very high. I could fall and not kill myself. The rough surface of the holds under my fingertips reassures me. This is an easy warm-up. I have climbed it a dozen times before. As I move, I feel my muscles tense and release with exactly the right amount of effort. Enough to get the job done, but not enough to wear myself out. Is that how it felt for Carlos when he climbed Turtle Alley? There's not a lot of space in my mind for thinking about Carlos—or anything, really. It's just me and the wall—reaching, stretching, pushing, pulling—until six moves later I'm at the top, both hands on the final hold. One glance behind me, and I drop down to the mat. I let the momentum of the fall push me onto my backside and all the way over, until I come to a rest with my shoulders on the mat.

I raise my head to look over at Lissy, just about to haul herself around the overhang. It's not as elegant as when Carlos did it, but she makes it, and he slaps the ground. "Awesome!" he says. Lissy finishes the next couple of moves without a problem.

"What's next?" she asks when her feet hit the ground a few moments later. I start to answer but stop myself, because she's not looking at me. She's looking at Carlos. And by the way he's looking back at her, I know neither of them will even notice if I go and get a drink.

By the time I return, wiping water off my chin with the back of my hand, they have moved into the bat cave. They are having a contest to see how many moves they can make upside down before they fall off the ceiling and onto the crash pads below. Their laughter is even louder than the sound of their bodies thumping onto the mats. I head for the far end of the bouldering zone so I don't have to listen.

## Chapter Three

Lissy is hanging by her fingertips from the fingerboard fastened above her bedroom door. She shifts her grip and pulls up until her eyes are even with the top of the door frame. "One. Two. Three. Four. Five." Slowly she lowers herself, moves her fingers to new holds and then pulls up again. I would be rushing through the counting, but Lissy seems to be in no hurry.

I find a place to sit on her bed between her neatly organized piles of camping gear. "When are you leaving?"

"Four. Five." This time she eases herself all the way down. "We'll leave right after school Friday, set up camp in the dark and come back late Sunday night."

It seems like a lot of effort for a couple of days of shivering in the woods. But for Lissy and her parents, escaping into the wilderness is what like going to church is for some families: an act of dedication.

"You should come," Lissy says, though she knows what my answer will be. "We're climbing on the back side of Bald Eagle Mountain."

I know it's beautiful up there, but I've never been. Maybe I'd tag along for a picnic. I might even camp. But climbing outside? Lissy knows how I feel about that.

Lissy shoves a puffy sleeping bag into a stuff sack. "You know your gym climbing would improve if you climbed real rocks, right?"

I pick up a climbing magazine from the top of Lissy's dresser. The cover photo is of a young woman hanging onto a steep cliff right beside the ocean. There's no rope. If she falls off, she will plunge into the water below.

"It would be way more fun if you'd come with us."

Maybe she's right. Maybe not.

"Competition climbing is not the same as rock climbing," she says.

"It's a complementary activity. Harder and easier at the same time," I say.

"How would you even know when you won't climb outside?"

Why do we bother to have this conversation over and over again?

"When you are climbing a mountain," Lissy goes on, "you don't really have the option of freezing and getting lowered back down. Not without messing up everyone's day."

The magazine smacks against the dresser louder than I mean it to. "That's not fair."

"No? It's too easy to give up in the gym. At least, when you're practicing."

It's true that I fight harder when I'm competing, even though I'm lead climbing, which is harder than using a top rope. My fear of falling is even worse, but somehow I usually manage to push through when the judges are watching. "I get to the top most times."

"If the routes are easy, yes. If it's one of your projects, and it gets a little tricky—"

"What's with you? Why do you care?"

"I'm trying to be helpful. I'm your friend, remember?"

"And it's helpful to tell me my climbing sucks?"

She punches the last bit of sleeping bag into the stuff sack and yanks the drawstring tight.

"You are a really good climber. You know that. You are amazing in competitions. But you forget that climbing in the gym on fake plastic holds is practice for actual climbing. Outside. On cliffs and mountains."

"That's not true! Maybe I like climbing inside where I don't have to freeze or get soaked or hike a million miles to even get to the mountain."

"You, Ayla, are full of crap. You are just too chicken to climb outside. And if you ask me, that's why you'll never be a really great climber. Don't look at me like that— I'm not saying that in a mean way. But since when were you friends with me because I just said what you wanted to hear?"

"I didn't ask you for your opinion. Have a great time at Bald Eagle. I'll see you in the gym on Monday night." I pull my phone out of my pocket and check the time. "I've got to go. I have that poetry project to do, and Dad wants me to help him..."

Lissy places the bulging stuff sack between her sleeping pad and a neatly rolled quick-drying camping towel. She looks at me with one eyebrow raised. I don't bother finishing my sentence. We both know my dad doesn't need help with anything and that analyzing a poem isn't going to take me very long.

I put my phone away. "It's my turn to cook dinner."

"Don't be mad," she says.

"I'm not." I want to add that maybe she should start making her own plans for her weekends instead of always doing stuff with her parents, but I don't have the energy to fight anymore.

## Chapter Four

On Monday, Lissy and Carlos sit side by side at one of the long tables in the lunchroom. Even from the far side of the room, I can hear Lissy laughing. Her long hair is loose over her shoulders, soft against the back of her thick handmade sweater. Some of the other kids from the climbing team are at a table by the window. Emily from my math class sits by herself at one of the smaller tables just past the end of the serving counter. Oh, right. I'm supposed to help her at lunch today. In my moment of hesitation, Lissy glances over her shoulder and sees me.

"Ayla! Over here!"

"Hi, guys," I say, sliding my tray onto the table. "How was camping?"

"Cold!" Lissy says and laughs. "But so worth it. Where we were climbing was south facing, so by the time we hiked up there to start, the rock was warming up."

I shake my head. "Nuts. That's all I have to say."

"I want to see this place," Carlos says.

"You would love it. There's this one place where the hang gliders go..."

Carlos spreads his arms as if he's flying. "Yes!"

"You're even worse than she is!" I say to him.

"You should hear what *he* was climbing on the weekend," Lissy says, leaning sideways and giving Carlos's shoulder a nudge with her own. They exchange looks as if they are wondering whether to tell me. "The back side of Liberty."

"Liberty?" I can't think of a mountain called Liberty.

"On Fifth," Lissy adds.

"Liberty Cinema?"

Lissy nods and gives Carlos an admiring look. Carlos takes a swig from his milk carton.

"What do you mean?"

"The back wall is huge," Lissy says, as if this fact justifies someone wanting to climb it.

"You climbed the wall of the theater?"

Carlos nods and wipes his mouth with the back of his hand.

"How?"

"Easy," he says. "It's brick. There's lots to grab onto, and once you get into a rhythm—"

"Why?"

"Why not?"

Carlos and Lissy exchange a look. Lissy couldn't be thinking of climbing buildings, could she?

"Carlos wants to go climbing at Black Dog next weekend."

"Black Dog?" I seem to have lost the ability to think of my own stuff to say. All I can do is repeat what they say. It's like my ears and my brain and my mouth can't quite believe what I'm hearing.

"Yeah, it sounds awesome," says Carlos. "I was thinking of free soloing. Check it out for hang gliding in the summer."

Climbers like to do the south face of Black Dog at this time of year for the same reason Lissy and her family climbed Bald Eagle on the weekend. When the sun has a chance to warm the rock, it's possible to climb even this late in the season.

"Depending on the weather," Lissy adds. As if the weather is the most important thing and not the fact that Carlos is even considering free soloing the climb.

"The whole thing? You'd do the whole climb with no ropes?"

Lissy leans forward and around Carlos so I can see her properly. "The climbing isn't that hard. Free soloing is a mind game as much as anything. You should try it sometime."

"You're not thinking of—"

Lissy laughs. "No. I'm going up there to do some work on the route with Dad. There's a couple of places that need cleaning. Moss grows crazy fast in the shade. And we'll do some trail maintenance on the lower approach."

I think of my own father lying on the couch at home. The curtains closed because he's afraid someone will look in and see him there.

"You going to come?" Carlos asks.

Lissy laughs, her head tipped back. "Don't even bother asking. Ayla only climbs in the gym."

"Seriously?"

"Some of us want to live long enough to be able to...to...vote."

"Vote? Yeah, because voting makes you feel alive," Carlos says with a grin.

"Leave her alone," Lissy says. "Nothing wrong with being a gym rat—right, Ayla?"

The way she says it, I can't tell if she's teasing me, defending me or throwing out a challenge. Suddenly I'm not very hungry.

"Do you guys want my lunch?" I ask, pushing my tray toward them. "I don't feel great, and I promised to go over the math problems with Emily."

"Lucky you," Lissy says. "She's right over there..." She nods to where Emily is still hunched over her tray.

I stand up. "Duty calls."

Carlos nods but isn't really paying attention anymore. He has pulled out his phone and is flipping through screens, looking for something. "Did you see this video about Alain Robert?"

"See you tonight at the gym?" Lissy asks as I'm walking away. I look back to answer, but she is already leaning over Carlos's phone. "Is that the French guy you were telling me about?" she says to Carlos.

"Yeah, I'll see you there," I say, but she doesn't answer. She doesn't even look up. And when Carlos slips his arm around her waist so they can sit closer to watch the video, she lets him.

## Chapter Five

At the gym, Carlos pulls a small notebook out of the zip pocket on the back of his chalk bag.

"Did you draw that?" Lissy asks, pointing at a spider on the cover. She stiffens a little. I know how much she hates spiders.

Carlos doesn't notice. "Yeah. It's in honor of Alain Robert."

"Who is this guy?" They both turn to look at me. "What? I've never heard of him."

"The French Spider-Man," Carlos says. "He climbs huge buildings, mostly without ropes or a harness or anything."

I imagine a skyscraper and the pavement far below. *Splat.* "Is he insane?"

Carlos laughs. "No crazier than I am."

There's a big difference between climbing the back of the theater in town and tall skyscrapers. Though I guess Carlos would be just as dead if he fell from the roof of the Liberty.

Lissy ties in to the rope and checks that my belay device is properly secured to my harness. "What's the tallest thing you've climbed?" she asks.

Carlos opens his notebook. The pages are filled with lists, numbers and dates.

"Four hundred and twenty-seven feet. The Great Western Bank building in Los Angeles. That was last summer."

"He doesn't just climb buildings," Lissy says. "He likes cranes and bridges too." She puts her hand on the first hold on the wall. "Climbing."

"Climb on. But what if you fall?"

27

"You can't fall if you don't let go." In his book he writes down the date and notes the route number and grade he's about to climb.

"You keep track of everything you climb? Why don't you use an app?" I ask.

"Habit, I guess. I started with a notebook before I had a phone. Besides, you can't draw on the back of your phone."

"I guess so. But I like my app—"

From halfway up the wall, Lissy adds, "So she can compare herself to other gym rats."

"Do you have a problem with that?" Tracking my climbs is one way to remind myself I'm not really getting worse, even when it feels that way.

Alex, a lanky climber wearing a baggy T-shirt, ambles into the gym, tugging the waist strap of his harness tight. "Sorry I'm late," he says to Carlos. "Hi, ladies, how's the climbing?"

Lissy reaches the top of the wall and rings the bell. "Awesome, Alex!" she says. "Lower!" I relax my brake hand so the rope can slip through my grip, and she begins to descend. Carlos only moved here a couple of weeks ago. Already he's made a bunch of friends, most of them climbers.

Alex and Carlos pick a route close by. Carlos ties his knot in the rope and secures it to his harness. Alex checks to make sure everything looks good. I wonder what Carlos thinks about having to use safety equipment in the gym—if it all seems like a big waste of time to him. He glides up the wall, easing his hips from side to side. His movements are as smooth and graceful as a dancer's. Watching him work his way to the top, confident and calm, I can't imagine why anyone would ever feel uncomfortable high above the ground. Not when the rope and harness and your friends are there to catch and support you. What's wrong with me?

I tie in and then check Lissy's belay device and carabiner.

"Locked," she says and touches my knot, nodding.

I turn to the wall, breathing easily. "Climbing."

"Climb on," she replies. As I start up, Carlos reaches the top of his route, and the bell tinkles.

"Lower!" he calls down. We pass each other when I'm partway up. "Looking good, Ayla!" he says.

"Thanks!" I answer and give him a big smile because I do feel good. Strong. I concentrate on placing my feet well and pushing up with my legs before reaching for the next holds. When I reach the top, I feel like singing or laughing or shouting something ridiculous like "Whoa, baby!" I don't do any of those things. I ring the bell and say, "Lower!" Push back and away from the wall and enjoy the ride down, swinging gently at the end of the rope.

"Good job," Lissy says. Carlos glances over from where he's belaying Alex. He nods and smiles.

"You'll be scampering up mountains before you know it," he says, his grin widening.

I smile back although, inside, my firm confidence has dissolved into jelly.

"You never know," I say. I turn to Lissy. "What's next? You going to try this one beside us or that horrible overhanging thing with the pyramid block in the way of the crux?"

"Let's go play on the pyramid. Carlos? You guys want to join us over there when you're done on this route?"

"Sounds like fun."

I haul on the rope, pulling it down from where it's threaded through the anchor at the top of the wall. "Rope!" I say, to warn anyone close by when the top end slips free and falls toward us. The rope hisses down and hits the mat beside me with a *thwuck*. Lissy grabs our water bottles and we head over to the nasty climb we've both been having trouble with. Even though Lissy's agreed to climb with me, it's obvious by the way she keeps looking over her shoulder that she's more interested in what Carlos is doing.

"Your turn," I say.

"Yeah," she agrees and ties in. It's only when she's on the wall again that I think she's actually paying attention to me. Then again, maybe she's imagining herself chatting with Carlos about climbing skyscrapers.

# Chapter Six

"Dad?"

I push open the door to our apartment and call out so I don't startle him. There's no answer, but the TV is on, so I know he's home. I drop my pack by the front door and kick off my shoes. It doesn't smell like anything is cooking for dinner.

"Hi," I say, poking my head around the corner. Dad's on the couch, his feet on the coffee table, watching some kind of court-room drama. His big toe pokes out of a hole in his sock. He turns his head a little, but his eyes don't actually leave the TV screen. "Pasta okay?" I ask.

"Thanks, honey." It's the script we follow almost every day. I wonder if he'd notice if I stuck my tongue out or gave him the finger. Right away I feel terrible for even having the thought. It isn't his fault.

It doesn't take long to chop up an onion and some garlic and sauté them while I wait for the pasta water to boil. There are a couple of leftover sausages from dinner the other night. I cut them into chunks, add them to the onions and then rummage around in the cupboard for a jar of pasta sauce. My mom would have made the sauce from scratch, but I like to think she'd forgive me since I'm at school all day. The wooden spoon slurps through the sauce mix, and I throw the pasta into the pot of boiling water.

As the pasta cooks and the sauce heats through, there's just enough time to set the table. Two place mats. Two spoons. Two forks. Two glasses. A jug of water. Even as

I plunk the Parmesan cheese down, I know there's a good chance Dad will carry his food over to the couch. Maybe I should join him. Except the couch is his domain, and the kitchen table is mine. This is where I do my homework, eat, read. I can see him from my place at the table, and somehow it makes me feel better to be able to keep an eye on him. Not that he's doing anything interesting, but still. I like to think he enjoys having me around.

"So, Dad," I say when the food is ready and he's making his way to the table. "I'm thinking about going camping with Lissy."

He hesitates, one hand on his plate and the other on his water glass. Then he pulls out his chair and sits down.

"Camping? I didn't think you were much of a camper. Where would you go?"

"Black Dog."

Dad stirs his food around so the pasta is evenly coated with sauce. "It's beautiful up there," he says. "When would this be?"

"On the weekend."

35

He lifts a forkful of food toward his mouth but then stops and stares at his plate. The fork sinks back down, and he picks up the Parmesan container, sprinkling a white layer on top of his meal. "Want some?"

"Thanks."

"This weekend?"

I nod, sprinkling some cheese on my pasta too.

"Who else is going?"

"Lissy's dad—you remember Andrei?" My dad should know my best friend's dad, but ever since the car accident, I never know what he'll need help remembering.

"Of course I know who Andrei is—for Pete's sake."

"And Lissy and another friend you don't know."

Dad eats a mouthful of pasta, chewing thoughtfully. "Thanks for dinner."

I wonder if he will ask who the other friend is and how I will answer. I don't know what he would think if he knew a boy was coming along. Maybe if I mumble he'll think I'm saying "Carla" instead of "Carlos."

"Will you be climbing?" he asks, not looking up.

"*They* will be climbing," I say. "And doing some trail clearing. I'll help with that. I was also thinking of taking my camera and a book."

He grunts. "I don't want to hold you back," he says. "But I don't know how safe that is. To climb mountains. Black Dog is a decent-sized mountain."

"I know. That's why I was thinking of taking the camera..."

"Won't you be bored? For a whole weekend? Won't you *want* to climb with your friends?"

I have no idea how to answer these questions. There is no right answer when it comes to climbing and my father. He worries about everything. He isn't even happy about me climbing at the gym. He complains every time he has to sign a permission slip for me to go to a clinic or competition. My coach is great about it. She tells him I have a lot of potential and that it's his responsibility to support me.

"I don't know what your mother would say. Maybe you should try to talk to her."

We both stop eating for a moment. It's a ridiculous suggestion. Mom is obsessed with other things—making heaps of money, her new husband and her troublemaking stepson, Mitch. To track her down between now and the weekend would be tough—she's three time zones away and travels a lot for work. When she *is* around, she's distracted by bailing Mitch out of juvenile detention and trying to spend quality time with her new husband. I'm pretty sure she couldn't care less about me going—or not going—on a camping trip. I'll save my "call Mom" option for an actual crisis.

"Lissy's dad will be there," I say. "If I do climb, it will be easy stuff, and I'll stay close to him." I don't mention that Lissy and Carlos would probably laugh at the thought of climbing anything easy. I sure don't say that chances are pretty good they wouldn't use ropes either. Lissy is getting more and more interested in free soloing and definitely more and more interested in Carlos. Which is the real reason I'm going. If I'm there, maybe I can stop her from doing anything too stupid. I've pretty much given up on the idea that Carlos would ever be into me.

"Why now?" Dad asks, surprising me a bit with his question. It's almost like he knows I'm not suddenly getting in touch with my inner Girl Scout. Obviously I can't tell him I'm worried Lissy will follow her new love interest up a cliff without a rope. He would never let me go.

I think carefully before I answer. "I don't see Lissy enough," I say finally. "I kind of miss hanging out with her."

He narrows his eyes a bit, and I wonder how much attention he's been paying to my comings and goings. It's true Lissy and I haven't been spending quite as much time together as we used to, but it's not totally accurate to imply our friendship is in terrible trouble.

"Good friends are important," he says. I wonder if he hears how ridiculous that statement is coming from his mouth. I can't even think of the last time he had a friend over or went out to do something fun. "Be careful," he adds. And then, "What about camping gear?"

We talk about what we have around the house and what I will have to borrow from Lissy. Dad doesn't ask any other questions about the trip. It never occurs to him to go back to the subject of the mystery friend who will be joining us. I am happy enough to focus on the packing list. As soon as we have more or less figured out what I'll need to borrow, I clear the dishes from the table.

Right on cue, Dad gets quiet and goes back to his place on the couch. He turns the TV back on and picks up his show where he left off.

# Chapter Seven

In the cafeteria the next day, Lissy pushes a list toward me.

"The most important thing on there is the fuel," she says. Then she adds, "I can't believe you're coming with us! That's so great!"

I scan the list. Other than fuel for the camping stove, I have to bring along my share of the food plus my own gear—a sleeping bag and pad and whatever clothes I will need. I guess *personal items* includes stuff like a toothbrush. Lissy and her dad are bringing the tents and all the ropes and outdoor climbing gear.

Carlos reads over his list. "Water purification tablets?"

"There's no running water there," Lissy says. "At least, not out of a faucet. There's a lake, but only an idiot—or a city guy like you—would drink from that without treating the water." She grins, and he laughs.

"Camper's Supply Store," I tell him. "Downtown."

"Yep—you could pick up the green soap too," Lissy says.

"Green soap?"

I'm glad Carlos is asking the question. I imagine a bar of green-colored soap like the stuff my dad uses.

"The stuff that biodegrades. Liquid. Comes in a little bottle—we don't need much."

"I can get all that at Camper's Supply?"

"Yep." Lissy grins at Carlos like they are sharing some big secret. She crosses the soap off her list and adds it to his.

"Hey, I have to go there anyway to get the fuel. Why don't I grab the soap and tablets at the same time?"

"Perfect," Lissy says, reaching over to cross the soap and tablets off his list. "Do you have a quick-dry towel?" she asks.

"No," Carlos and I answer at the same time.

"I'll bring two extras. Look and see if there's anything else you guys need. As long as I know in advance, we probably have something you can borrow."

"Her house is like a camping supply store," I say.

Carlos nods. "I know. I saw what she has in her garage."

Really? When did he have a chance to go over to Lissy's place?

"Did you know," I start to say, "that she was conceived in a tent, born in a–" but Carlos jumps in.

"Born in a gully and grew up in a backpack? Yes, I knew that."

Apparently, Lissy has covered all the important subjects already. Lissy's family is famous around here for being more at home in the wilderness than in town. They should have their own reality TV show. Lissy doesn't seem to hear us.

"Oh—I didn't put climbing stuff on your list, but obviously pack your harness and shoes and stuff. I'll bring an extra helmet for you."

"Thanks." I don't want to tell her that the chances of my climbing anything are slim to none. She'll just want to know why I'm coming if I'm not planning to climb, and I don't feel like outright lying. If she knows I'm mostly coming to keep an eye on her, she will un-invite me so fast...

"Carlos?" she asks, leaning toward him. "Do you have a helmet? We wouldn't want anything to hurt that gorgeous hair of yours..." They both laugh.

"Only an idiot would hang glide without a helmet."

I have to look away when she touches his hair lightly and then grins. It's like she doesn't know I'm still here at the table. Who am I kidding that I'll be able to make the least bit of difference when she and Carlos are together?

In town later that afternoon, I hop off the bus and head down past the coffee shop at the corner of Ralston and Main. Big splats of rain start to pelt down, so I break into a jog. If it rains on the camping trip, they won't be able to climb. If the weather is awful, will we cancel the trip? Or should I pack playing cards or something? Homework?

Seriously? What is wrong with me? Homework? What self-respecting sixteen-year-old would even consider putting homework on her packing list? But if it does rain, what will we all do? Where will we hang out? Will Lissy and Carlos try to sneak off into one of the tents to make out while I, what, go bird-watching or carve something out of a tree branch with Andrei? I am trying to wrap my head around the horrible things that could happen if the weather is bad when the Liberty Theater comes into view. The back wall of the building is imposing in a way I'd never noticed before. Straight up, it's unbroken by any kind of ornamentation. The bricks are neat and orderly, the gray-white lines of mortar smooth and even.

And they are smooth. I touch one, pushing my fingers into the groove between two bricks at shoulder height. The space can't even be called a crack. I look down at my feet. I'm wearing street shoes, but I find it hard to believe that even with climbing shoes there'd be enough room to get a useful toehold. I look up. Gray clouds scud low over the buildings. Rain pelts down at me, heavily enough to be seriously annoying. Way up at the top, a giant spider has been painted across the wall.

It's clever—beady-eyed and hairy. More sophisticated than you'd expect, considering where it is. Did Carlos take spray paint up with him? Surely he didn't use brushes. It must have been him. Did he do it when he climbed up from the street? Or did he hang from a top rope? When I squint, the spider looks like it might be moving. It must have been Carlos. What was he thinking? Did Lissy help him? Keep watch? Lower him down from the roof?

A gust of wind sends an empty paper coffee cup scooting along the sidewalk. I pull my sweater close and move on. It's another two blocks to Camper's Supply, and by the time I get there, I'm pretty wet. It doesn't take long to find the stuff I'm supposed to get. I grab a cheap plastic rain poncho too, the kind you stash in your emergency kit. Bright orange. It's not exactly stylish, but it will get me to the bus and from the bus to my house. And, I guess, I could dry it out and try to fold it up small again and take it along. At least if it does start to rain while we're away, I'll have a bit of extra protection so I don't have to spend every minute hiding out in a tent.

# Chapter Eight

When we arrive at the parking lot closest to where we will be camping, it's pouring out.

"Nice view," Lissy's dad says, pulling a tight-fitting wool hat down over his ears. I roll my eyes. There is no view. Thick clouds sit low and heavy, pushing down against the tops of the trees. Mountains? What mountains?

When Andrei kills the engine, the rain hammers down on the roof of the truck. "You guys still up for this?"

Carlos laughs. "This is going to be fun!"

Is he serious?

"*And* I can tick a summit off my list." Carlos has been talking about how he wants to climb eighteen mountains before his eighteenth birthday next summer. The only one who thinks this is a crazy idea is me. Lissy and her dad think it's cool he's so excited about mountains. They've been offering suggestions ever since he brought it up.

Lissy is beside me in the backseat. She leans forward and reaches between the front seats for a bag of peanuts. "Want some?"

"Sure." I pop a handful into my mouth and chew. She doesn't ask if I want to stay out here in the middle of nowhere in a downpour. Though what choice do I have? It was a two-hour drive over a winding mountain highway from town to the turnoff. After that we bumped along something more like a donkey trail than a road. Ours is the only vehicle in the parking lot.

"It's not that cold," Lissy says. "It's supposed to stop raining overnight. We can climb on the south side tomorrow afternoon. When the sun comes out, the rock dries pretty fast."

"As long as I get to the top, I'll be happy," Carlos says. "Fastest way up, even if it's a bit wet."

"Not going to happen," Andrei says, suddenly serious. "This isn't like climbing at the gym. Wet rock is no fun."

Carlos stares at the rain running down the windshield.

"Don't look so miserable. We can still get to the top. There are hiking trails up the back side. It's longer to go that way, but the view is just as good. That would give us a chance to work on the upper part of the trail."

A hike sounds like a better idea than trying to climb anything. If we all help Andrei with some of the trail clearing he has planned, we can feel like we accomplished something.

"Hear that?" I ask. The rain has slowed a little.

"Once we get moving, we'll be okay," Andrei says. "Like Lissy said, it's not actually that cold. Dress in layers. You need to stay as dry as possible, but once we get going you'll warm up pretty fast."

Lissy passes me another handful of peanuts. "Ready? Let's do this. We've still got a long way to go before we can camp."

I'm not keen to leave the warm, dry truck, but the other three have their doors open, and the damp air seeps inside. I open my door and step out into the drizzle.

It takes longer than I expect to pull the packs out of the back of the truck and sort out who will carry what. There are the climbing ropes, the bolting tools and hard-ware, the tents and the food. We also take a curvy tree saw, a folding shovel and a small ax. I never thought much about who helped keep trails in good shape for hikers. Us, apparently.

I have one of the ropes and the folding shovel. Andrei helps me settle my pack onto my back. I'm shocked at how much heavier it is now.

We spread my new rain poncho over both me and my pack.

"You look like a pumpkin!" Carlos says.

"You'll wish you had one when you crawl into a wet sleeping bag later tonight," Lissy says. "Why don't you use this?" She pulls a big garbage bag out of the back of the truck.

"I'll be fine," Carlos says.

"Seriously—you will be much happier if you at least start out dry." Lissy doesn't wait for him to agree but uses her penknife to cut a hole in the bag for his head and two smaller holes for his arms. "Here you go."

Reluctantly Carlos pulls the makeshift rain gear over himself. The fit is terrible—too tight across his chest and his arms poke out sideways like a scarecrow's.

"Very stylish," I say, feeling smug about my own bright-orange gear.

Lissy and her dad don't have to worry. Their fancy packs have built-in rain covers that stow away in hidden pouches when they aren't needed. When we're finally all ready, Andrei locks the truck and heads for the trailhead.

"How far to the campsite?" Carlos asks, shifting his pack.

"Two hours or so," Lissy answers. "We'll have plenty of time to get there, set up camp, get a fire going and eat before dark."

Andrei has already set off down the trail. Two hours. When we were talking about the trip, that didn't sound like much. But now my back and shoulders are already feeling the weight of my pack. Water is dripping off the front of my flappy rain poncho and onto my jeans. Two hours seems like a very long time to be marching along in the rain.

At first the trail is wide and level. We follow the gravel path alongside a stream, swollen and gurgling after the recent rains. We are still in the forest, and above us thick cloud hides the mountains. We have only been walking for ten minutes or so, but with Andrei and Lissy setting a quick pace, I am soon hot and sweaty under all my layers. Lissy and Andrei don't break stride, but unzip the tops of their waterproof jackets.

Carlos is breathing hard. His face is flushed, and sweat trickles down his neck. "I can't go two hours like this. I'm losing this garbage bag."

"Wait," Lissy says as he starts ripping a hole in the front of the garbage bag.

"What?"

"I was going to suggest you just put it over your pack. Your jacket should keep you warm enough."

"That's a better idea," Andrei agrees. We all stop on the trail, and Lissy and her dad fuss around, pulling and tucking the torn garbage bag around Carlos's pack.

Standing still and shifting my weight from foot to foot is even worse than hiking with my pack. At least, that's what I think until we set off again. Then I realize that hiking doesn't feel any better. I glance behind me. We can't see the parking lot, but it feels like it's still close enough to reach without too much trouble. With every step we take along the trail, that feeling fades. By the time Andrei finally suggests we take a break, half an hour or so later, I feel close to desperate. What was I thinking? Why does anyone volunteer to do this sort of thing? What kind of fun is it to be damp, sweaty and exhausted, with an aching back and sore feet, and still not be anywhere close to your destination?

## Chapter Nine

Our rest stop doesn't last long. The rain has settled into a light misting drizzle. At times, the sky brightens a little, though the clouds don't break. We are all warm, and we each peel off a layer, stuffing sweaters and hoodies into our packs and putting our rain gear back on.

Carlos pulls a bag of potato chips out of his pack. "I'm starving." He tears into the bag and takes a handful. Passing the bag around, he licks his fingers and grins. "Food of the gods."

We take swigs from our water bottles, and then Andrei glances up at the sky. "Let's keep moving," he says, shouldering his pack.

Lissy and Carlos follow suit.

"Let me give you a hand," Andrei says, noticing I haven't moved. He heaves my pack up, and I back into the shoulder straps. I don't even have time to finish snapping the buckles closed on my waist and chest straps before the others start hiking. Still fumbling to buckle up, I follow along, trying not to trip.

The trail is narrow now. We wind around and over tree roots and rocks. Slowly the trail starts to climb, and it isn't long before I am really hot. "Can we stop? I need to get rid of another layer."

The others are dropping their packs at the side of the trail before I've finished asking the question. "Tie that on the outside," Andrei says to Carlos, who is about to stuff his jacket inside his pack. "You might need it again, and you don't want the dry stuff in your pack to get wet."

The rain has finally stopped, but the clouds are still low, and I wouldn't trust the weather to cooperate. I tie my plastic poncho to the outside of my pack.

"Have a quick drink," Andrei says, though it isn't necessary. I'm already pulling out my water bottle. It's more than half empty. I calculate how much I should drink now and how much to save for our next couple of stops before we reach camp. I've read those terrible survival stories where six people on a life raft have to share half a cup of water for seventeen days. I can't even imagine the stress. I started off with a full bottle and only need to survive a two-hour walk from the parking lot to the campsite. Yet all I can think about is if I'll have enough water. I decide on three big gulps and stash my bottle away.

We set off again. The grade here is suddenly much steeper. It's important to concentrate on every step. The trail has narrowed to almost nothing, and now we are picking our way over slabs of rock and chunks of stone. Some are stable enough to step on. Some wobble precariously. In places, it would be bad news to slip off the side of the trail. Even worse than how wobbly I feel with each step is how desperately I need to go to the bathroom. I guess that's another downside of consuming too much of your drinking water too fast. The need to pee is overwhelming.

The rain starts again as we struggle up to the top of a long, open section of trail. As we crest the ridge, we all stop. Below us, a valley holds a lake right in its center. All around, mountains rise up. The clouds have lifted a little and are starting to break. Shafts of sunlight stream through a jagged hole in the clouds. The sunshine catches in the raindrops and the air is filled with a million tiny rainbows.

"Sun-showers," Lissy says. "They're good luck."

The tops of the mountains glisten with a dusting of fresh snow.

"We're not climbing up that high, are we?" I ask.

"Nope," Andrei says. "We'll be heading over there." He swings his arm to the left and points at a cliff face jutting up out of what looks like a massive rock pile.

"That's Black Dog," Lissy says.

Andrei nods. "See the waterfalls? Those are Black Dog Falls—Upper and Lower." A series of waterfalls cascades down the rock face. "It doesn't look that far away, but getting to the approach will take about two hours from camp. We'll hike over there in the morning and check out the rock, see how dry it is. Most likely we'll hike around to the right." He moves his arm in a curve, following the line of the mountain's flank. "That's where the hiking trail starts."

The straps on my pack dig into my shoulders. It's a good thing we won't be carrying all our gear up there, but even so, I'm thinking tomorrow is going to be exhausting.

"Let's press on," Andrei says. "I'd like to get camp set up sooner rather than later."

Nobody argues. With the valley meadow in sight, our spirits have lifted, and we set off in a more enthusiastic mood than we have been in all day. Half an hour or so later we reach the lake, and as we lower our packs to the ground for the last time, the sun blazes through a big opening in the clouds. The ground steams and the lake water glistens.

"How do you like it so far?" Lissy asks.

"It's beautiful," I say. And it really is. I draw in a deep breath. The mountain air, clean and fresh, fills my lungs. Lissy and I start setting up our tent in just our T-shirts. Maybe this camping trip won't be so awful after all.

## Chapter Ten

"Here, I'll hang this up," Lissy says, fiddling with a small light. She fastens it to a loop inside the top of our tent. It isn't bright, but more than enough to light up the small space of the tent. I dig through my pack in search of the pair of sweatpants I brought along to use for pajamas.

"How is it possible to lose something that big in a relatively small space?" I say.

"Your packing system is terrible. Light

is right. Dual purpose for everything. Efficiency is—*ow!*"

My tattered copy of *Harry Potter and the Philosopher's Stone* hits her on the shoulder. Lissy picks it up and waves it at me. "Perfect example right here. Like you're going to have time to read this."

"I might—"

"You won't. Though if you tear some pages out you could start a fire."

I snatch the book back. "Never!"

"Dual purpose for everything," she says again.

Everything about camping takes way longer than I expect it to. By the time darkness falls and we've finished clearing away the dishes and brushing our teeth, I'm exhausted.

It isn't even late, but I feel like I've run a marathon. Reading before bed is the last thing I feel like doing. Instead, I burrow down into my sleeping bag and curl into a ball to warm up.

"Good night," Lissy mumbles from her bag.

"Good night," I answer, and a minute later I am sound asleep.


It's pitch dark when I wake up. Somehow my sleeping bag has slipped off my shoulders, and I feel like I'm inside a deep freeze. It can't be that cold, but even after I wiggle back down inside the cocoon of my bag, I can't warm up. My toes are the worst. I rub my feet together, but it doesn't help. I don't know what Lissy was talking about when she said I'd stay warmer without any socks on. Wrong. Wrong. Wrong.

Opening the top of the bag only wide enough to let one hand out, I feel around beside me for my pack. Cold air seeps into the little space and chills the back of my hand. Groping for my socks, I find a pair of gloves. They will have to do.

It's awkward to reach down inside the narrow sleeping bag and wiggle my feet into the gloves. But Lissy would be impressed at my resourcefulness—dual purpose for everything. My feet don't even squeeze halfway into the gloves, but at least my toes have another layer on them. Not that it helps much. I shiver and close my eyes, trying to pretend that I'm at home in my bed, snug and warm. A drink would be great, but we didn't bring any food or drink into the tents. Everything remotely edible is hanging from a tree to protect it from animals. Even the toothpaste is tucked away inside the food bag.

At home, I often get up in the middle of the night and slip out into the kitchen to get a glass of water. On my way back to bed, I usually go to the bathroom. Why did I have to think about home? And a flushing toilet? Now I really need to go. The more I think about it, the more I am convinced my bladder is going to explode. The choices aren't great. I could pee in my sleeping bag—but that's just disgusting. Or I could hold on until dawn. Maybe. Or, I suppose, I could go outside in the pitch dark, with wild animals all around, and risk freezing to death while I find a spot to drop my pants and do my business.

The longer I lie here thinking that I might survive until daylight, the more I realize there's no way I'm going to make it. I reach out of the sleeping bag for my sweater, drag it inside and squirm into it. Then I sit up and pull on my jacket and woolen hat. I already have my sweatpants on, and I decide against trying to squeeze into a second pair of pants. This is going to be a short trip. But socks—I will need socks, as the gloves have already come off down in the bottom of the bag somewhere.

It takes me a full five minutes to find my spare socks and pull them on. Finally, I am ready to venture outside. Through the whole process of getting ready I've tried to be quiet, but it's hard not to make noise with a rustling sleeping bag and zippers loud enough to wake the dead. Fortunately, Lissy's deep breathing never changes. She is sound asleep and doesn't stir until I tug at the zipper of the tent door. The sound is like a chainsaw ripping through the night.

"Where are you going?" she mumbles from inside her bag.

"Bathroom."

"Don't get lost."

"Sorry I woke you."

There's no response beyond more deep breathing. How is it possible she can sleep so soundly?

Outside, I straighten up and take a deep breath. The night air is crisp and chilly. I swing my arms in big circles to try to warm up. I forgot to grab my flashlight, but I can see well enough to make out the other tent, the dark water of the lake and the shapes of the mountains looming all around us. Above me, the stars look as if someone has taken a handful of fairy dust and flung it across the sky. When I breathe out, my breath hangs in the still air. Nothing moves. It's so quiet, the loudest sound is my own breathing.

I don't dare go too far, but I move away from the tents and the lakeshore before I drop my pants and squat behind a bush. The whole process only takes a couple of minutes, but by the time I unzip the tent again and crawl back inside, I am much colder than I was before I set out. Wiggling back into my sleeping bag, undressing and pulling the bag tight over my head is almost as awkward in reverse. Even with socks on, my feet are still cold. There's no way I'm going to fall asleep.

I shift around from side to side, trying to find a comfortable position. Is it possible to suffocate inside a sleeping bag? My breathing quickens. It's warmer with my head inside the fabric. But even though I try to reason with myself that a sleeping bag isn't anything like a plastic bag, and that I'm in no danger of actually dying, my heart starts pounding. The next thing I know I'm thrashing around, pulling the bag away from my face. I suck in lungfuls of air as if I've just surfaced from a deep dive.

Why can't I sleep the way Lissy is sleeping? She's snoring softly now, like a bear cub or a puppy. If I match my breathing to hers, will it help? Sleep might be out of the question, but at least I can relax and rest a bit before the day begins. A day of hiking. Or climbing. Thinking about tomorrow only makes things worse. What if we get lost? What if the weather turns awful again? What if we run into a bear? What if Carlos does something stupid and falls off a cliff? What if? What if?

## Chapter Eleven

"Hey—wake up, sleepyhead!"

Lissy pokes me through the sleeping bag. I blink. The tent glows.

"It's gorgeous out here. The sun's out! Come on—breakfast is ready."

I sit up, still a little confused about what's going on. How did I fall asleep? "What time is it?"

"Breakfast time!"

Lissy is only half inside the tent. She is fully dressed and has obviously been up and about for a while. She's grinning, her head and shoulders reaching in far enough to be able to poke me again.

"Okay! I'm awake—I'm up."

She backs out, and I pull on my sweater and jacket. I wriggle out of my sweatpants and into my jeans, lying back to pull up the zipper and fasten the snap. When I crawl out into the sunshine, I'm actually feeling warm.

Andrei and Lissy are squatting by the tiny stove, stirring something.

"Oatmeal," Andrei announces.

"With raisins," Lissy adds, as if it's the most delicious treat. "There should be enough coffee left in the pot for you to have a cup. No milk though, so you'll have to drink it black. There's some sugar in that container."

I'm not usually much of a coffee drinker, but the thought of something hot is appealing. I add a spoonful of sugar to the miniature tin cup Andrei hands me and take a sip. The coffee has already cooled to a temperature just better than lukewarm, but I take it gratefully. Yuck. Disgusting. How can people get so attached to this stuff?

"Where's Carlos?"

Both Andrei and Lissy point toward the lake. Carlos is a little farther along the shoreline, splashing water on his face.

"Cup empty?" Andrei asks.

"Not quite."

"Drink up—you'll need the cup for your oatmeal."

Dual purpose for everything. I guess it makes sense not to carry any more than is absolutely necessary. I drain the last bit of coffee and hold out my cup.

"There's enough for a couple of helpings each," Andrei says as he dishes out a modest portion. Lissy and her dad dip their spoons into the cooking pot. When Carlos joins us they put a bit of oatmeal into another drinking cup.

"Delicious!" Carlos says with a big grin. He blows on the steaming spoonful of oatmeal and watches the steam rise. "I filled the water containers—that pump-filter thing takes forever!"

"Better that than getting sick," Andrei says. "You put the tablets in as well?"

Carlos nods and eats his oatmeal, smacking his lips and rolling his eyes. "Oh, that's so good!"

"Eat up!" Andrei says. "Have a piece of fruit too. As soon as we're done, we'll pack up and get going."

It seems to take forever to reorganize everything at camp, hang up the food that we won't be taking, make lunch and decide who will carry what. By the time we've finished, the sun is still out, but high clouds drift across the sky.

"I have a basic first-aid kit in my pack," Andrei says. "Carlos and Ayla—you two can each take one of the larger water bottles. That should be plenty for the day. Lissy—you're okay with a rope and the lunch?"

Lissy nods. "You're going to take all the draws and stuff?"

"Yeah, I've got it," Andrei says. He peeks inside a drawstring bag before putting it into his daypack. For about the hundredth time, he looks up at Black Dog as if the mountain can tell him what the day will bring.

"It looks like the upper cliffs—the more exposed rock—are drying out. By the time we hike up there, we should be able to climb okay. Down at the bottom here—see where it's still shady?"

We all look where he's pointing. It's harder to see because the lower part of the mountain is still in the shade, but the darker color of the rock could easily be dampness. It's hard to tell from this distance.

"I doubt that's going to be climbable—maybe tomorrow, if the weather holds and we don't get any more rain."

I wonder if I should "accidentally" forget my harness. I could avoid climbing, but then it sounds like I'd be stuck somewhere up there if the others did decide to climb.

"Make sure you've got your harness and helmet," Andrei adds. "You can clip your helmet to the outside of your daypack if it won't fit inside." Andrei sounds like my science teacher running through an instruction list before one of our chemistry labs. The fact that he knows what he's doing and has a plan makes me feel a tiny bit better. He isn't going to do anything stupid or dangerous. If he says it's safe to climb, then it's going to be safe to climb.

"Dad? Are we taking all three ropes?" Lissy asks.

Andrei considers her question for a moment and then nods. It's like he's been reading my mind. "If we all wind up climbing up there, we'll need three ropes. We'll also take the ax, the folding saw, the clippers and the small shovel so we can work on the trail."

I fasten the folding shovel to the outside of my pack, straighten up and press my hands into the small of my back. My load looks like it belongs to a gold prospector. "I don't know how much climbing I'll do. But I can take photos of you guys," I say, touching the camera strap slung around my neck.

"Are you okay?" Andrei asks.

Suddenly worried they might leave me alone at camp, I quickly add, "Yes. Yes—I'm fine. A little stiff from sleeping in the tent last night. That's all."

At least if I change my mind once I'm up there, I can blame my sore back and not have to admit I'm the worst kind of climbing wimp imaginable.

Carlos stops as we scramble up and around a massive boulder and arrive at a slightly wider section of the trail. It's been hard work getting this far. Between cutting and dragging away branches and tree roots and moving rocks to make steps and hauling our stuff ever higher on Black Dog's lower slopes, I'm already tired. I'm glad we've mostly been in the shade, because I'm sweating hard.

"I need to lose another layer," Carlos says.

Nobody argues. We're all breathing heavily. Our daypacks, though lighter than the full packs we carried into camp, still weigh enough to be uncomfortable.

They land on the hard-packed, rocky trail with a series of thumps.

Free of our packs, we start pulling off whatever clothing we can. Lissy and I are down to our tank tops, and her dad has on a short-sleeved, quick-drying shirt. Carlos pulls his shirt up and over his head and Lissy shrieks. "Oh my god!" She points at Carlos, but we all stare at her. Apparently, she has lost her mind at the sight of his impressive muscles.

Carlos grins. "Meet Arania."

He turns around so I can see what has Lissy so rattled that she is pressed against the massive boulder beside us.

A large, very realistic spider is tattooed onto the back of his shoulder. Its two front legs look like they are reaching up and away from his skin. The spider's glossy black body is round and full. Two curved pincers at the front of its head look ready to pierce the skin at the base of Carlos's neck.

"*That* is a cool tattoo," I say. "It's a lot like the one on your notebook—" I glance at Andrei and stop myself before mentioning the giant spider on the back wall of the Liberty Theater. I suspect Andrei wouldn't be too impressed to know he's in the company of a vandal.

"I designed it." He's trying to sound like it doesn't matter, but I can tell he's kind of pleased his creation is making such an impression. Though not with Lissy. She shudders and inches away along the wall.

"Spiders," she says. "Yuck. How can you sleep at night with that thing crawling over your skin?"

Carlos laughs. "It's not going anywhere. It's not like I can feel it—or see it even. Come say hi to Arania! You can touch her—she won't bite."

Andrei clears his throat.

"Don't worry, Dad. I'm not going anywhere near that thing."

"Hey," Carlos says. "Who are you calling a thing?"

We all laugh, but Lissy doesn't come any closer. For as long as I have known her she has been terrified of spiders. We can laugh about it when there are no spiders around, but more than once she has screamed loudly enough when some poor, innocent spider has wandered into sight that I've shrieked in sympathy.

"The shoulder straps will cover her up," Carlos says, lifting his pack.

"You stay ahead of me," Lissy says, "so I can keep an eye on you and your terrible pet."

"What? In case she decides she doesn't like me anymore and comes to get you?" Carlos extends his wiggling fingers toward Lissy, who lets out a squeal.

"Stop!" she says. "I'm serious. I have a thing about them..."

"I never would have guessed," Carlos says.

# Chapter Twelve

"We should keep moving," Andrei says, and a few minutes later we are back in single file, picking our way through and around rocks as the trail gets steeper. Soon I have to grab at rocks to help pull myself up. The trail has changed from being something to walk along and is now something to climb. We scramble up and over and up and over, moving steadily higher up the flank of the mountain. At least here there's less brush to clear.

When we stop again, Andrei puts his finger to his lips and says, "*Shh.* Can you hear that?"

We all hold our breath and listen. "The waterfalls!" Lissy says.

"Once we get around that next corner we'll be able to see Lower Black Dog Falls. We can stop there for a snack and a drink."

"Sounds good," Carlos says.

We move a little quicker, and for the next few minutes we are all quiet, intent on getting to the falls. When we arrive I feel instantly refreshed. More alive. I tip my head back and suck in a deep breath.

Lower Black Dog Falls splashes down from high up on the side of the mountain. I can't see where it begins. The noise at the bottom is so loud we have to shout to be heard. Spray hangs in the air, and the sun catches the suspended droplets. Everything shimmers.

I'm glad I brought my camera. I experiment with the settings, slowing the shutter speed so the water looks like a smooth, soft, white cloak over the face of the jagged rocks.

I try to zoom in on the sparkling droplets, but I can't seem to capture the way the sun makes the tiny prisms glitter.

"Are you going to eat?" Lissy shouts.

"Coming!"

Lissy and her dad have spread out quite a feast on a slab of rock far away enough from the falls that it is dry. Carlos is already filling a piece of soft flatbread with chunks of tomato, slices of bell pepper, cheddar cheese and shredded lettuce. He spoons on some salsa from a plastic container and then folds the wrap neatly around its contents.

We do the same and find places on nearby rocks to sit and eat. We don't talk. The waterfall is mesmerizing. For nearly half an hour we snack, enjoy the sun and explore the area at the bottom of the falls. I don't know about the others, but I'm not in a rush to keep heading up the mountain. According to Andrei, the trail gets steeper from here. Seriously? What does he consider the bit we've already hauled ourselves up?

"The next section is tough scrambling, but it isn't that long. After that we can cut back over to the south face and see if we can do some climbing. If the sun stays out, the rock should be dry enough. We should have a couple of hours of good sun before we're in the shade again and have to think about coming down."

When we pick our way back out onto the trail, I look down into the valley. Our bright orange and green tents look like toys beside a painted lake. Occasional high clouds scoot across the sky, and the surface of the lake changes as dark patches shift its color from turquoise blue to something more gray and ominous.

There isn't much time for sightseeing. Andrei sets a brisk pace. If I want to avoid falling off the narrow lip of the trail running along the top of the scree slope below us, I need to pay attention. Below me and to my right is about a thousand feet of rubble. The jumbled rocks have fallen down from the high cliffs above us. It doesn't surprise me when Andrei stops and makes us put on our helmets. Our skulls protected, we continue to make our way along the base of the cliffs. I can't stop thinking about how all those rocks below us, tons and tons and tons of debris, must have tumbled from somewhere high up on the mountain above. Did they come down in one big rockslide? Or a few at a time, a million times over? Either way, it seems impossible that these looming, solid mountains could be slowly crumbling away.

"This looks good here," Andrei says, craning his neck to look up at the rock face above us. "It's mostly dry. Hey, I wouldn't go too far without being tied in," he adds, giving Carlos a stern look.

Carlos is at least twenty feet off the ground, both fists jammed into a crack. "I'm okay," he says. I don't know how he can sound so calm. My heart thumps just watching him.

"I don't need to be rescuing anybody today." Andrei opens his pack and starts pulling out his gear.

Carlos hesitates for a moment and then starts to climb down. He leans away from the cliff, extending his arms straight out, fists balled up and jammed into the crack. That way he can see where to put his feet. He moves one foot at a time down the rock, finding somewhere secure enough to steady himself. Sometimes that's in the crack, sometimes on small ledges to either side. Once his feet are set, he relaxes one fist and eases his hand out of the crack. He lowers his body so his knees are bent and finds a new hold for his free hand. Then he repeats the process for his other hand. After both hands are securely wedged into the crack, he leans back away from the wall again and then moves his feet down a little farther. He never hesitates and never seems out of balance.

While I am mesmerized by Carlos easing backward down the cliff, Lissy and her dad are busy getting ready for Andrei to start climbing up. This is a long route, so our ropes aren't nearly long enough to reach all the way to the top. We will climb in sections, or pitches. Each pitch will have a bolted anchor at the top, but between anchors there is nothing to clip quickdraws to. Quickdraws at the gym are fastened permanently to the wall. Those Andrei will use have two carabiners, one at each end. On this wild cliff face, there aren't any bolts to clip one of the carabiners to before snapping the rope through the carabiner at the other end. Andrei needs to find or create places to attach his quickdraws to the mountain. Not everyone is crazy enough to want to free solo like Carlos. I can't imagine who would want to climb without using protection, no matter how good they are.

"There are bolted anchors higher up," Andrei says. "I'm going to check them as we go. They should be in good shape, but I do have everything I need to replace any that look sketchy. I'll let you know if I have to start drilling."

As Andrei talks, he pulls all kinds of trad climbing gear from his pack. He organizes his bits and pieces by type and size and then snaps everything to gear loops on his climbing harness. I can't even imagine how he's going to use some of the stuff. He has several long strips of strong webbing sewn into loops of different lengths, some clipped to his gear loops, a couple slung across his chest. "Pass me the nuts, Lissy."

At first I think he's hungry. Then Lissy hands him a set of assorted odd-shaped lumps of steel attached to short loops of wire cable.

"Now the cams."

One at a time she passes him things that look like gears. He tests each one as he takes it, pulling a lever and watching the gear ends expand and contract. The smallest nuts are the size of my pinky fingernail. The bulkiest cam is bigger than my fist.

While Andrei is getting everything organized so he can find it in a hurry, Lissy stacks the climbing rope so it will run out smoothly as her father climbs. Belaying for a lead climber out here is a whole lot different than protecting someone who is climbing at the gym.

Andrei straightens up and then ties one end of the rope to the front of his harness. Lissy has already set up her belay device, threading the rope through it and finding herself a good place to stand where she can see what her father is doing. They check each other's setup and then Lissy says, "On belay."

Andrei nods and turns toward the rock, his collection of gear like a strange steampunk miniskirt bristling around his waist. "Climbing."

He climbs at least fifteen feet above us before setting a piece of protection, a midsize nut he slips into a crack. When he's happy with the angle it's wedged at, he tugs at the end with the loop of cable to make sure it's set. Then he snaps a quickdraw into the loop. As he reaches down in front of him to take hold of the rope, Lissy is ready to make sure he has enough slack. The second, lower carabiner clicks as he snaps the rope into it. The whole maneuver takes less than a minute, and he is climbing again.

He repeats the process, finding a place to put protection. When the cracks and small openings in the face of the cliff are too big for nuts, he uses a cam. When he squeezes the lever, the gears at the other end are small enough to fit in the space. When he lets the lever go, the gears fan open and wedge the device tight. He snaps a quickdraw into place, pulls up the rope and climbs again. After Andrei has placed about a dozen pieces of protection, Lissy shouts, "Ten feet left!"

"Okay!"

Andrei's upward movement slows and stops. He eases up and over a ledge about 150 feet above us, and we lose sight of him.

## Chapter Thirteen

There's a long pause and not a sound from Andrei.

"What's taking so long?" Carlos asks.

"He's probably checking the anchor to see if it's sound." Lissy keeps her hands on the rope and looks up at the spot where Andrei disappeared.

I had put on my harness when the others did, but the longer we stand around, the faster my heart races. What if Andrei is having some kind of problem up there? How would we even know?

"Secure!" Andrei shouts from some-where above us.

Lissy unclips her belay device. "Off belay!" she yells back.

The rope slides upward as Andrei pulls at the other end.

"That's me!" Lissy yells when she feels the rope tug at her waist.

Andrei stops pulling and a moment later he shouts, "You're on belay!"

Lissy has fastened one end of each of the other two ropes to the back of her harness so that when she climbs they will trail behind her. "Make sure they feed out smoothly," she says.

"This would go a lot quicker if I just climbed—" Carlos begins.

"Forget it," Lissy says. "You're using a rope. Dad would never let you climb without. See you up there soon. Climbing!" she calls out and starts up. "You might as well tie in to the other ends so you're ready to go."

As Carlos and I watch Lissy climb, we keep the ropes uncoiling smoothly and manage to get our own knots tied. It seems like Lissy has only just left when we hear her call out from above.

"You're on belay, Ayla!"

A moment later Andrei yells the same thing down to Carlos.

Carlos glances at me and then answers for both of us. "Climbing!" He places his hands on the rock.

I can't see how I can get out of this now. It's not that different from climbing in the gym, I tell myself. I'm secure on a top rope. Carlos said he will clean the gear Andrei put in on his way up. I don't even need to worry about that. It's going to be fine. Just fine.

"Are you okay?" Carlos asks, looking over at me.

I clench my teeth and force myself to nod. They can't leave me here. It's bad enough seeing the ropes go up and over the ledge, even though I know Andrei and Lissy are just out of sight. It would be terrible if they all completely disappeared and left me alone.

"On belay!" Andrei shouts again. I guess they have noticed we haven't made any progress.

"Climbing!" I call back, though my voice sounds small and weak. I am so nervous I think I'm going to wet my pants. I glance down at the knot on the front of my harness. There's no slack in the rope at all. I take a deep breath and start to climb. Carlos moves off the ledge at the same time and we move upward together, more or less staying side by side.

At first I can hardly think straight. But then I find a kind of rhythm. Unlike at the gym, I don't have to wait to grab a particular-shaped hold. The cliff might have seemed blank when I was standing back and looking up, but the minute I place my hands and feet, holds appear everywhere. Some aren't that big, but they are enough to pull against and wedge my toes into. And they are everywhere. The surface of the rock is like a rich tapestry of grooves and bumps, cracks and ledges.

"Look at you go!" Lissy shouts down from above me. When I glance behind me I am shocked at how far I've already climbed.

Carlos gives me a thumbs-up. "Wait a second while I get this," he says, reaching sideways to wriggle out a nut Andrei had wedged into a narrow crack. As he shifts his weight onto his right foot, something breaks, and a piece of rock tumbles away behind him. "Rock!" he shouts as he pops off the cliff and swings sideways, caught by the rope from above.

"You okay?" Andrei shouts.

"Yee-haw!" Carlos answers, hanging from his rope. Then, looking at me, he says, "I'm fine. Let's keep going." He grabs onto a little outcrop with one hand and places his feet back on the cliff. "That was fun. Hey—I'm fine. You should try falling every now and then. Maybe it wouldn't scare you so much."

I don't bother to answer. It takes all my willpower to make myself push on. A few minutes later my head pops up over the ledge and I see Lissy and Andrei grinning back at me. Carlos is right beside me.

"Welcome!" Andrei says as I step up and over the edge to join them. "That's it. Come over to my other side where there's some room."

Room? There's a whole new definition of space when you are trying to cram four people onto a narrow ledge 150 feet up in the air. The spot Andrei is pointing at isn't even wide enough for me to stand unless I turn my feet sideways. Even then, my hip presses into the rock. Compared to the tiny lips, ridges, bumps and cracks that have just passed for toeholds, though, the ledge feels as big as a couch! I can't help grinning as Carlos heaves himself up and over the edge to stand beside Lissy.

"Go ahead and put your locker there." Andrei points to a big carabiner he has fastened to two slings of webbing suspended from two bolted anchor chains.

I snap my locking carabiner into his, and then he shows me how to make a double hitch knot to fasten myself to the wall.

After Carlos secures himself to the anchor, Andrei says, "Thanks for cleaning. Any time you want to give me my gear back..." He laughs as Carlos and I look at each other and then down at Carlos's harness. Of course. Andrei will need his gear to protect the next section of the climb.

Carlos unsnaps carabiners and detaches draws from cams, nuts and slings. He passes the gear to Andrei, who clips everything back to the gear loops on his harness.

"What happened down there?" Andrei asks Carlos.

"A piece of rock broke off right as I was about to clean the nut."

"That's why it's insane to free solo," I say.

"I wouldn't have been off balance and I wouldn't have trusted that foothold," Carlos fires back.

"You *do* climb differently on a top rope," Lissy says.

Is she seriously defending him?

Andrei is quiet as he organizes the ropes and checks that everyone is well secured to the anchor.

"Dad used to free solo all the time."

"You did?" I thought Andrei had more sense. And now it's too late for me to go back and find a safe, warm rock to nap on.

"In Yosemite," Lissy goes on. "Right, Dad?"

"That was before I was married. Before we had you."

"I don't have any kids," Carlos says. "Don't plan to either."

Lissy and I laugh, though Andrei's face stays serious.

"I'm responsible for you today," he says, sounding more dad-like than I've ever heard before. "So you're going to use a rope. You don't have a lot of mountain experience, and these conditions aren't ideal. There are still some slick patches, and the rock around here isn't always the most stable."

"Yeah. I noticed," Carlos says. "No problem. I appreciate you letting me come.

I want to climb out here more often."
He waves his hand in a broad sweep that
takes in the panoramic view of mountains,
valley and lake.

"It's hard to beat, that's for sure," Andrei
says, collecting the last of the quickdraws.

# Chapter Fourteen

Before long, Andrei is ready to go again, and he and Lissy repeat the same process from the ledge. Now, though, Lissy is fastened to the anchor as she belays him. She leans back, coils of climbing rope draped across the taut sling in front of her waist. The hardest part of the second pitch is a tricky piece of rock that bulges out from the cliff face. At first I can't see how I'm going to get up and around the lump. Several times I get stuck halfway, awkwardly scrabbling with my foot trying to find a place to push against. I back off to a small ledge just below and off to the side.

"Carlos, you'll have to do this first." Lissy and her dad had both navigated the obstacle so smoothly that I didn't notice what they did.

Carlos makes his way to where I've stalled out. "I think they both reached up and around for a hold on top," he says. "I can't quite see it." He wedges one foot into a corner under the bulge of rock. With one hand flat against the cliff face, he uses his other foot to lever himself up and over the outcrop. As he swings up and around, his right hand reaches for the hidden hold. He times it perfectly so that he grabs it right at the peak of his move upward.

"Good job!"

"Your turn," he says, moving out of the way.

I wedge one foot into the corner like he did and think about the physics of what I need to do. There's always a moment—the deadpoint—after you jump up and before gravity yanks you back down again. It's like when a basketball player goes in for a layup and seems to hang in the air before firing the shot and dropping back to the ground.

The first time I try, my thrust is strong enough that my fingers graze the hold, but I don't quite make it. Lissy is keeping the top rope snug from above, so I don't fall anywhere. Instead I just bump against the block and stop.

"Try again," Carlos says. "Push a bit harder with your feet and really commit to the move."

I focus on the sequence—right foot in the corner, left palm on the wall, strong push off with the left foot—up, look, reach, grab.

"Yes!" Carlos says as my fingers close on the bit of rock I need to find.

Then I'm past the overhanging block and moving up the rest of the pitch beside him.

We climb three more pitches using the same system. Andrei leads, Lissy follows him, trailing two ropes, and Carlos and I bring up the rear, cleaning gear as we go. With each pitch, I get a little braver and offer to work free some of the protection so Carlos doesn't have to do it all.

We settle into a comfortable rhythm. Andrei only has to replace a single bolt—as he'd suspected, the existing anchors were in good shape. Carlos climbs a little more carefully after his fall and doesn't come off again. Eventually, I've relaxed enough that I'm able to concentrate on the climbing. Now that I know it's impossible for me to escape without going to the top, there isn't much point to panicking. In some strange way, it's a relief to know I'm stuck up here.

"This one's the easiest pitch of the day," Andrei says at the bottom of a section that looks like a series of narrow ledges. It's not quite as vertical here. The mountain feels like it's leaning back a bit, though higher up I can see it gets steeper again. "After this, just two more to the top. But this one will go fast—which is good, because we don't have a whole lot of daylight left. Everyone doing okay?"

We all nod. After Lissy and her dad run through their routine checks again, Andrei sets off quickly and confidently.

"Want to place some gear, Dad?"

Andrei is well above us, higher than he usually goes before placing some protection. "I guess I should," he says, pausing just long enough to place a nut, clip the draw and move on.

"I hate it when he runs it out like that," Lissy says, her face stern. We all watch the length of rope trailing behind Andrei get longer and longer. "Dad!" she shouts. "You'll hit the ground if you come off!"

"I'm not coming off," he says, but he stops again to put a beefy-looking cam deep into a crack.

Lissy doesn't take her eyes off him. We're all looking up at Andrei's progress. My neck is feeling pretty stiff. I can't even imagine how Lissy must feel when she climbs all day with her dad. Her neck must be killing her.

"Don't you ever get tired of—"

One moment I'm seeing Andrei moving across the face of the cliff, making his way toward a useful-looking crack over to the left. The next there's a weird, loud noise from high above us. It's like someone has smacked the mountain with a giant open hand. Andrei's head snaps up and he yells, "Rock!"

We all dive forward, tucking in as close to the cliff face as possible. I hunch my shoulders, press my helmet against the cliff and jam my hands over my ears. The noise is crazy for a few seconds as we are showered by a storm of rocks. I don't dare look to see how big the rocks are, but judging by the noise of the rubble crashing down behind us, some of them must be huge.

Carlos shouts, "Rock! Rock!" as if we haven't already noticed we are caught in some hideous hailstorm of stone and rubble. Clouds of dust choke the air.

Lissy is to my left, and when I peek over, she suddenly lifts off her feet as if she's flying. I reach out to grab for her arm, but she is flung aside with such violence that I am knocked backward and nearly lose my footing on the ledge. "Lissy!"

Above me there's a dull thud, and Lissy screams. I have never heard a noise like that come out of a person before. It's a noise that's part terror and part pain.

It's all over in a few seconds. The sound of falling rocks is replaced by the skittering of pebbles slithering down around us. After a moment even that has stopped. Instead I hear Lissy gasping. Carlos and I raise our heads at the same time. We are both spattered with mud.

"Lissy—are you—?" It's obvious she is not okay. She moans, suspended above us, managing to hold herself still against the rock by hanging onto the crack with one hand. With the other she has a death grip on the rope below her belay device. One foot is braced against the slab of the cliff face, and the other leg dangles at a bizarre angle below her. Even from here, I can see it must be broken.

"Dad? Dad? Say something!"

Andrei hangs like a rag doll above her, still moving like a massive weight at the end of a pendulum. As his swinging slows, his gear scrapes across the rock. Blood drips out from under his helmet and across his forehead.

"Andrei!" Carlos and I shout together. Andrei does not move. When he fell, his weight and momentum must have lifted Lissy right up off the ledge. Caught by her tether to the anchor, she slammed into the wall.

"What happened?" Carlos asks.

"I don't know," Lissy says, her voice shaking. "He yelled *rock* and I looked down, because it was like half the mountain was falling on us. I didn't want to get knocked out. Oh my god my leg hurts." She is puffing now, taking short little breaths and closing her eyes.

"Lissy. You have to get down from there. Can you lower yourself?"

"We have to get Dad down," she says.

"We can't do that until you get down yourself," I say.

"I'm going to pass out," she says. "It hurts so much." She has turned a horrible shade of pale gray.

"Lissy? Did you hurt something else? Did you bang your head?"

There's a long pause as she looks down at me and then up at her dad hanging at the other end of the rope.

"Are you bleeding?" I can't even think of the right questions to ask. Whatever first aid I might have known has flown off the cliff along with the falling rocks. I don't remember anybody ever talking about what to do if both accident victims are hanging somewhere out of reach above your head.

## Chapter Fifteen

"Lissy," Carlos says. "Lower yourself down with your belay device." His voice is slow and calm, as if he's speaking to a little kid.

Lissy looks up at her dad again. "We have to get him down," she says. "Dad!"

Carlos tries again. "Lissy! Listen to me. You need to let go of the crack and get both hands on your belay device. We need to get you down first so we can lower your dad. Do you understand what I'm saying?"

She doesn't answer but turns her head slowly to look at the hand that's hanging onto the crack.

"Use your good leg to keep yourself off the wall. Let the other one hang down. Don't try to use that," Carlos says.

"I can't. It hurts so much just to breathe."

"We need to get your dad down here," I say, but she doesn't seem to hear me. "Lissy—listen to Carlos. Do exactly what he says. We'll help you when you get close enough that we can reach you. Okay?"

"Lissy—let go of the crack," Carlos repeats. "You need both hands on your device. You need to control your descent. You don't want to drop yourself or your dad, right?"

That's what I've been thinking, but I can't believe Carlos has said the words out loud. I don't dare look back over my shoulder. We have climbed a long way. We must be six hundred feet above the next piece of ground that's anything close to level. And that was the big flat area where we organized our gear at the bottom of the first pitch.

Carlos and I stare at the white knuckles of Lissy's left hand clinging to the crack. Slowly she eases her hand back. As soon as she lets go, her body swings sideways. She tries to get her good leg onto the wall, but she is so off balance that her injured leg smacks into the rock. "*Ahh!*" It's not a word—it's another animal noise, and it cuts right through me.

"You're okay," Carlos says. "It hurts, but you're not going to die from a broken leg."

I look back up at Andrei, still hanging limp in his harness. The way he hangs it's as if he's lying on his back but suspended by his belly button. His head lolls to one side, and his legs are bent at the knees. His back is slightly arched, and his arms flop down below him.

Lissy squeezes her eyes shut and gives us two quick nods. For a minute, I think she's going to try to find something on the wall to hang onto again. But then her left hand moves to join her other hand, which is still firmly gripped around the rope. Even during the fall and the rockslide, she somehow managed to hang onto the rope on the bottom side of the device. She would have to be dead before she'd let go of her brake hand.

"Now go very, very slowly," Carlos says, "so you don't jerk down."

Inch by inch, Lissy starts to lower herself. Carlos and I reach for her, and when she sways as her good foot touches the ledge, we each grab an arm and steady her.

"Can you put any weight on it at all?" Carlos asks.

"No—she shouldn't even try," I say. "She could hurt it more."

Lissy bursts into tears. "Even just hanging down it hurts," she says between sobs. "What are we going to do?"

"We need to get your dad down from there," I say, looking up at Andrei. "Can you sit while you lower him?"

It's already crowded on the narrow lip of the rock, but at the very end there's a spot wide enough for Lissy to sit if she lets her good leg hang over the edge.

There's no room for both of us to help her. I'm closer, so I get a good grip on her arm, and she shuffles along sideways, whimpering and crying every time she moves and her leg swings a little.

"Carlos, take the break end for a minute so Lissy can hold on to me. That's it. Okay, Lissy, I'll help you sit. Good."

I try not to think about all the space behind me. I'm still tethered to the anchor, but if I slip over the edge, I could get banged up. That's all we would need.

Lissy sinks to the ledge, taking a dozen deep, shuddery breaths in the time it takes her to move from standing to sitting. White lines streak her face where tears have run down her cheeks through the dirt.

"Okay?"

She manages a nod and takes back control of the rope.

"Start lowering. We'll pull him in to the ledge when we can reach him." I turn and sidestep back along the ledge until I'm beside Carlos. We both crane our necks and watch as Andrei floats down toward us. The cliff is almost vertical and pretty smooth. As Lissy lowers him, his flopping limbs brush against the rock, which makes him turn first in one direction and then the other. He bumps against the wall but doesn't respond at all. Could he be dead? The thought is too awful to consider seriously. Then again, if he is dead we could leave the body and at least get ourselves out of here. The moment I have that thought, I feel like a murderer. He can't be dead. He just can't.

I'm at Andrei's feet and Carlos is at his head as he comes down toward the ledge. "Stop there," Carlos says to Lissy when her dad is just above the ledge. Carlos reaches over and undoes the straps on Andrei's pack. He pulls it off and hands it to me, and I jam it behind me. "Keep lowering," Carlos says.

Andrei is awkward and heavier than I expect. It's a good thing he's not a big man. His hips just fit onto the rocky shelf. Carlos pulls one arm across Andrei's chest, which, I'm relieved to see, is rising and falling. Andrei's other arm sticks out sideways over the ledge. Carlos tries to bend it at the elbow and fold it across Andrei's chest as well, but it flops back out again.

I have better luck with Andrei's feet and legs. As he drifted in for his landing, I was able to grab the leg farthest from the cliff face and push it onto the ledge. So far, anyway, it's staying put.

"Andrei?" Carlos asks. "Hey—can you hear me?"

We both watch his face intently for any kind of response. But nothing moves. No fluttering eyelids. No twitch of his mouth. Nothing. A trickle of blood seeps out from under his helmet.

"Dad! Is he breathing?"

"He's okay. He's breathing," I say.

"What are we going to do?" Lissy asks, sobbing again.

Carlos and I look at each other over Andrei's still body.

"Should we take his helmet off?" I ask.

"Maybe?" Carlos says. He leans out wide so he can see Lissy. "Lissy—you know more about emergency first aid. What else should we do?"

Lissy wipes her nose with the back of her hand. Her crying slows, and she leans her head back against the wall. Just when I think she isn't going to offer any suggestions, she says, "Pinch him."

"*What?*" Carlos and I say together.

"Pinch him—"

"Why?"

"Maybe he'll respond to that—it would be good if he did."

I don't want to ask what it means if he doesn't.

Carlos squeezes Andrei's arm. Nothing.

"Not like that," Lissy says. "Really hard." Now that she has pulled herself together, her color is starting to look a little better. Her bossy personality is recovering too. "I would do it myself, but it's not like I can walk over there."

Carlos doesn't look too happy, but he tries again, this time giving Andrei a really hard pinch on the arm. It's hard enough that it leaves a red mark when he lets go. Even better, Andrei moans.

"That's a good sign," Lissy says. "Dad! Can you hear me? Are you okay?"

We all hold our breath and stare intently at Andrei. Nothing.

"You should roll him onto his side," Lissy says.

"What if his neck is broken?" Carlos asks.

"Oh crap," I say. That hadn't occurred to me.

Lissy doesn't answer right away.

"He could choke if he lies on his back. I don't think we have much choice. Carlos, can you try to hold his neck steady? Ayla, can you roll him over?"

Yeah, maybe if we were on a flat surface somewhere. But here? There's no room to get behind him and push. I doubt I can even reach him from where I'm crouched at his feet. Even if I could get behind him, if I roll him over he's going to go right over the edge!

"What if you step off the ledge?" Carlos says, gingerly moving his hands to either side of Andrei's neck.

"Are you joking?"

"No. You're attached to the anchor. If you step over to his side—over there, beside and below him—then maybe you can get behind his hips and grab his harness. I can't really help if I'm holding his head."

"Oh. I guess so." Immediately below the ledge there is nothing but air. I'll have to plant my feet against the cliff face and sort of squat. "Lissy, can you get the rope to your dad tighter if we can roll him up on his side?" She is still holding on to the rope running through the belay device.

I adjust the length of my leash by moving the clove hitch until I have enough room to step backward over the edge.

"Don't step on him!" Lissy says.

"I won't!" I snap back at her. My heart leaps in my chest as I step back awkwardly, being careful not to kick Andrei. When my waist is level with the edge, I get a good grip on Andrei's harness and wriggle my other hand under his hip. "Ready?"

Carlos counts to three, and I push and lift while Lissy takes up the slack.

Carlos steadies Andrei's head and neck as he turns him toward the wall. Andrei moans.

"Andrei? Can you hear me?"

"Was that another moan?" Lissy asks.

"Maybe. Or maybe just a deep breath," Carlos says.

Cautiously I let go of Andrei's harness. He settles back slightly, but with Lissy taking up the slack, he is definitely more on his side than on his back.

"You'll have to tie him off there," Lissy says. "To the anchor. I can't hold on to him for...forever."

## Chapter Sixteen

I scramble back up onto the ledge. With Carlos still squatting at Andrei's head, I fasten two slings together so they are long enough to reach the anchor. I hitch one end to Andrei's belay loop. Andrei stays tipped onto his side.

"Now what?" Carlos asks.

"Can we call for help?"

Carlos pulls out his phone. "No signal."

"Someone has to go for help," Lissy says.

"Who?" Carlos and I ask together.

Lissy lets out a long sigh, as if she can't believe we've asked such a stupid question. "Well, obviously I'm not going anywhere, and Dad's not very useful. So you two will have to go for help."

"But—"

"But what? Do you have a better idea?"

Carlos holds his phone up in the air, as if that will make a difference. "Do you remember the last time we had a signal?"

"Almost back at the parking lot there's a spot," Lissy says. "Kind of where the lookout over the creek is. If you miss it, there's usually a signal at the parking lot."

"The parking lot? Like, where we parked yesterday?" I ask.

"You know that as well as I do, Ayla. You were the one complaining you couldn't get online in the tent."

"Yes, but—what time is it?"

Carlos looks at his phone again. "Later than I thought. And look—the sun is almost down behind the mountain."

In that moment, watching the shadows grow longer across the valley floor, the reality of our predicament hits me. We are in deep trouble. Nobody is going to be looking for us because nobody is expecting us back until late tomorrow night. So the earliest someone might start searching would be Monday morning. By then, it could be too late...

"Can't we lower you guys down?" I suggest. Surely it would be best to get us all off the mountain.

"Are you insane? We have no idea if Dad has a broken neck or how hard he hit his head. We haven't even looked at whatever is going on under his helmet. I won't be of any use—I'll just slow everything down. You two need to go down together as fast as possible."

"It doesn't make sense for us to leave now," Carlos says quietly. "It's too late. It's going to be dark in, what, half an hour? An hour at most? We don't know what we're doing. We don't know where we're going. So we'll get stuck somewhere halfway down or get lost, and then what? We should stick together tonight, right here. Then Ayla and I will leave at dawn."

The idea of the four of us spending a night on the ledge is horrifying. Anything would be better than that. Maybe Carlos and I *should* leave now. We have two head-lamps with us. We could leave one with Lissy and her dad on the ledge, and Carlos and I could take the other. Lissy, though, is already in survival mode.

"You're right," she says to Carlos. "What do we have in our packs for warm layers?" She makes a move as if to reach for her pack and gasps, falling back against the rock, pain tightening her jaw muscles.

"Do we have something we could use to make a splint?" Carlos asks.

It takes a moment for Lissy to compose herself enough to answer. "We should see what we have with us," she says. "Not just for a splint, but clothing, food, water..."

This can't be happening. Water. Shelter. Food. Those are things you think about when you are wondering whether you will live long enough to see another sunrise.

Everything is awkward on our shelf above nothing but air. As the sun sinks deeper behind the mountain on the other side of the valley, the shadows lengthen, until the valley seems dark and even farther away. Before long our ledge is in deep shade. It feels like the temperature has dropped by ten degrees. It can't be that much, but our first priority is obvious. Stay warm.

Carlos and I dig through all the packs and pull out whatever we can find in the way of clothing. We each add an outer layer, take off our helmets, pull on wool hats and put our helmets back on. The last thing we need is for someone else to take a rock to the head.

Andrei had been working harder than any of us, and when he fell he was only wearing a T-shirt. I find a fleece pullover and a puffy jacket in his pack and inch over to where Carlos is squatting at Andrei's head. "How are we going to do this?"

"Carefully," Carlos answers.

"Don't move his neck," Lissy says from her perch at the end of the ledge.

"I don't think that's going to be possible," I say. "But we can't leave him half dressed like this."

"Andrei? We are going to put some warmer clothes on you—okay?" Carlos speaks like he's talking to a very young child, drawing out each word and speaking much louder than he has to. There's no response from Andrei, who still lies facing the cliff.

"We can get this top arm in okay," I say, unzipping the fleece. "Hold his neck while I..." The first arm is easy enough, though I have to brace one leg against the rock face to get close enough to pull the sleeve all the way on. "There's no way I'm going to be able to get the other arm in..."

Carlos has one hand on each side of Andrei's neck. "Yeah. I don't think it's a good idea to try to sit him up or anything."

"You can't leave him like that," Lissy chimes in.

Obviously not. I don't answer her though. "Can you hold him still and maybe get your foot under his shoulder to lift him up a bit? Maybe I can wrap the fleece around and at least push the other sleeve underneath him."

Carlos gets reorganized, raising himself on one knee. He hunches over to keep his hands steady and then squirms awkwardly to get his other foot under Andrei's shoulder. He flexes his foot and takes some of Andrei's weight off his side. I'm ready to push and poke at the fleece, squeezing it underneath. I can't believe how heavy Andrei is. I reach over him and fish around for the sleeve and tug it underneath his body. I do what I can to smooth it out and pull it into place, tucking it into his climbing harness so it doesn't come loose. Carlos grunts with the effort of holding the cramped position.

"Repeat?" he asks.

We do the whole half-dressing maneuver again with the puffy jacket and tuck everything in as well as we can.

Then we turn our attention to finding some kind of splint for Lissy.

# Chapter Seventeen

"This will work," Carlos says, holding up Andrei's folding hiking pole.

"Good call," Lissy says. "There should be some bandage tape in the top of my pack. And some painkillers."

Carlos passes Lissy a small bottle of headache pills and a water bottle. "Take a couple of these right away," he says. "It might help to give them a few minutes to start working before—"

All three of us look at Lissy's leg. Dried blood smeared over her knee is visible through a hole torn in her pants. "Do you know where that came from?" I ask warily.

"My leg?" Lissy answers. It's hard to tell if she's making a joke.

"I mean, if it's just scrapes from the rock, that's okay, but if the bone is sticking out somewhere—"

"Oh man," Carlos says. "Do you know how to make a tourniquet?"

"I would have bled to death by now," Lissy says. "But no, I haven't looked at where it's broken."

We aren't going to be able to take off her harness and then her pants. So, very carefully, we pull back the edge of the torn fabric and try to peek inside. She flinches and closes her eyes. I can't see far enough below her knee to get an idea of exactly where her leg is broken.

"I guess we should cut that off?"

"No," Lissy says with a moan. "I need both of my legs."

"Not your leg—just the bottom part of the pants. They're ruined anyway."

"Yeah. Yeah—I knew that's what you meant," Lissy says. I'm not sure that's exactly true, but when Carlos hands me a penknife, I start to slice at the fabric. It's harder than I expect to cut the pants without cutting Lissy. Every time I touch her pants or brush against her leg, she yelps and twitches.

"I'm trying to be gentle," I say.

"I know," she whispers.

"Maybe it would be easier if you didn't watch," I suggest. At first I think she's going to argue, but then she closes her eyes and leans her head back against the rock.

"This makes an emergency room seem like a luxury hotel, hey?" Carlos says.

"Hurry up," Lissy says. "It's drafty down there."

I saw at the fabric a little more vigorously. When Carlos gently peels back the loose flap, any hope that we are only dealing with a sprain evaporates. Halfway down her shin, it looks like Lissy has grown

128

another knee. One that bends in the wrong direction. Carlos lets out a small shocked noise and then clears his throat. "At least the skin isn't broken," he says. "That blood is just from where you scraped your knee. No big deal."

Lissy lifts her head and has a look. One glance is enough. She leans back again and stares up at the cliff above us. "Oh yuck." She swallows hard a couple of times, and I wonder if she's going to be sick.

"Hey," I say, taking her hand and giving it a squeeze. "You'll be okay. We'll make a splint, so at least you can't make it worse by—" By what? Dancing? Hiking? Climbing back down the mountain? "By, um, falling asleep and bumping it or something."

"I can't believe we have to spend the night up here," she says as Carlos lays the hiking pole gently alongside her leg.

"We're going to have to touch it a little when we put the tape on," I say. "I don't know how else to—"

"It's okay," she says. "Just do it as fast as possible."

I pull out a length of tape from the roll and stick the end to the hiking pole. I pull the tape across the front of Lissy's leg just above her knee and then Carlos reaches to lift the leg so I can pass the tape underneath and start wrapping. Her scream is loud enough that it echoes across the valley. "Sorry!" Carlos says and drops her leg. Even though it only falls an inch or so, Lissy screams again, even louder.

"You ass!" she says.

My hands shake so badly that I drop the roll of tape. Thankfully, it doesn't fall far, because the loose end is still attached to Lissy.

She braces one hand against the cliff, panting. "I'm sorry," she says to Carlos. "I know you didn't mean to do that." Her other hand flutters in front of her like a wild bird not quite sure where to land.

Carlos reaches for her hand and holds it. "Hey. Crap. I'm sorry," he says. "Breathe. Breathe slowly. You're okay."

How can he sound so calm?

"Are you okay?" he asks me.

"I guess so. How else can we do this?"

"Knock our patient on the head with a rock so she can't scream like that?"

It's a ridiculous joke, but all three of us laugh. Even though they are small laughs, somehow it helps.

"Any ideas?" I ask Lissy.

She doesn't respond for a minute. "Yeah, maybe you *should* just cut off the leg. That might be less painful than splinting it."

"You two are hilarious," I say. "Seriously—"

"Try tearing shorter strips of tape and tack the pole just from above," she suggests. "Then add more tape closer to where it's broken. Maybe if it's a bit more stable, you could lift it and get some tape all the way around?"

She doesn't sound at all certain that this strategy will work any better.

"And I know now how much it's going to hurt, so I'll try to be quieter. And even if I scream again, keep going—I don't think you can make it much worse."

I don't know about that last part, but I'm game to try again.

"What if you chew on something? Like in the old cowboy movies?" Carlos asks.

"Like a bullet?" Lissy says.

"Exactly."

"I think those cowboys always had rum to guzzle," she says.

"That was pirates," Carlos says. "Cowboys prefer whiskey."

While they are joking back and forth, I tear off several strips of tape and tack the hiking pole to the side of Lissy's leg. She winces but doesn't say anything.

"Biting on something might be a good idea," I say, ripping a longer strip. I'm ready to try wrapping it around her leg again but terrified of what kind of noise she'll make.

Carlos reaches into his pack. "Here," he says and hands Lissy a sock.

"You want me to bite on a dirty sock?"

"It's clean," Carlos says. "I had a spare pair in my pack. Ball it up and bite down hard. I'll count to three so you can be ready."

To my surprise, Lissy balls up the sock, rolls her eyes and opens her mouth. Carlos counts slowly to three. Then, at the same time, Lissy bites down on the sock, Carlos lifts her leg, and I slip the strip of tape underneath, just below the break. Lissy still manages to make a terrible noise, but it's muffled and more like a deep groan than a scream. I have just enough time to pull the tape under her leg and get it stuck onto the pole before Carlos lowers the leg, and we pull the tape securely over the top.

"One more," Carlos says. "Okay?"

I tear off another long strip of tape and hold it up when I'm ready. Carlos counts to three again and we repeat the process. "I don't know what else to do," Carlos says.

We all stare at Lissy's useless leg stretched out awkwardly on the ledge in front of her. "My knee is cold," she says. For some reason, this strikes me as very funny. I laugh out loud, not the quiet little chuckles we've been sharing up until now, but a belly laugh that starts somewhere deep inside and just won't stop.

At first Lissy protests. "That's not funny!" But before she can even finish the words, she's laughing too. And when she starts, Carlos starts, and for a few minutes we are all laughing hysterically. Like we are just having the time of our lives hanging out together on the side of a cliff.

When the giggles slow down, Carlos takes the sock back from Lissy. He tries to pull the torn fabric of her pants over her exposed skin and then gets his other sock out of his pack. He ties both together and makes a sort of patch, which he lays over the hole. "Tape, please," he says seriously.

"Yes, Doctor," I reply. I tear off two more pieces so he can tack the sock patch over the torn pants. Carlos rocks back on his heels and admires his handiwork.

"My shoes are killing me," he says. It's only when he says it out loud that I realize how much my feet hurt. Rock shoes are tight, and we've been wearing ours for a long time. "How are your feet, Lissy?" he asks.

"Horrible," she says. "Can you help me put my approach shoes on?"

It's this quiet request for help that makes me realize how vulnerable she is. I wasn't expecting her to be able to hike off the mountain and get help to rescue us all. But the thought of her not even being able to sit on a ledge and change her shoes is horrifying in a whole new way.

# Chapter Eighteen

After we've changed our shoes and arranged ourselves in a row on the ledge, we use the last of the daylight to do an inventory of our supplies. We have two small bags of trail mix—about a handful each—one wrap, three cookies, two apples and three granola bars. We have a little more than a quart of water between two water bottles.

"How long does this have to last?" Carlos asks. I've seen how much he can eat.

The small pile of food would barely make a decent snack for him.

"We'll need to keep some here for me and Dad," Lissy says, "but we won't be doing anything, so we won't need too much. You two will be doing all the work—but you should be able to get to somewhere you can use your phone before the end of tomorrow. You'll be hungry, but you won't starve to death or anything."

"And we only need enough water to get back to camp. The purifying stuff is there. We can refill." Carlos is still looking at the food.

Lissy nods. "Water's heavy too—it will slow you down. So only take a small amount of water between the two of you, and leave the rest with us."

"I am so hungry," he says. "We should eat."

"You're right," Lissy says. "Pass me a headlamp. At least I can do this much." She switches on the light and opens one of the trail-mix bags. "One for you, one for you, one for Dad and one for me..." she says and counts out individual nuts. Then she picks out a raisin for each of us.

"This is going to take forever," Carlos complains.

"What else are we going to do up here to pass the time?"

"Chew slowly," I say. Even though we share only half a bag of trail mix, an apple and a granola bar divided into three, eating it at the speed of snails takes us almost half an hour. The meal feels like it lasts an eternity. When we're done, I'm shivering and still hungry. No doubt about it, it's going to be a very long night.

At first it seemed like it would take forever for the sun to completely disappear. In the end, darkness falls suddenly. As soon as our ledge is cloaked in black, the chill in the air develops a bite. My nose runs, and though I squirm and try to get comfortable, I hardly dare to move in case I fall off. I know I am still tied in and that my knot isn't going to spontaneously unravel, but there is something awful about not being able to see that everything is still correctly fastened where it should be. Tentatively I touch the climbing knot at the front of my harness, tracing the figure-eight pattern with my fingertips. Then I pull my hand back. What if I fall asleep and have a dream that I'm back at home and don't need my harness on anymore? What if I untie my knot while I'm sleeping?

The thought sickens me. Shifting sideways, I try to lean against the cliff but jerk upright when I realize how far sideways I am able to tilt.

"Carlos," I say softly. "Are you still awake?"

"Are you kidding me?" he answers. "Of course I'm awake. What's up?"

"Do you have the headlamp handy?"

"Yep. Do you need it?"

"Could you have a look at the anchor? It feels like my tether is really loose."

At the other end of Andrei's prone form, Carlos shuffles around. Gravel crunches under his feet, and the blaze of the light beam shoots in my direction. "Ow!" I say, shielding my eyes.

"Sorry." He shines the light on the anchor.

"Could you shorten me up a bit?" I ask.

He leans over Andrei, the headlamp illuminating the complicated-looking tangle of ropes, slings and carabiners fastened to the anchor. If the anchor bolts break or pull out, all four of us—plus the packs we have clipped into the ropes—will tumble off the ledge and disappear. Part of me hopes that if this happens, it will be when I'm sound asleep. Another part of me thinks that would be about the worst nightmare a person could have. Then again, the chances of my actually falling asleep on this rock are slim to none.

"How's that?" he says after some grunting and soft swearing. He balances on one foot so he can reach the clove hitch and adjust it without stomping on Andrei.

I lean sideways and right away am caught by the tight rope leash. "That's better. Thanks."

The light clicks off, and we are plunged back into darkness. It seems even darker after having been blinded by the headlamp.

"It's going to be okay," Carlos says. "By this time tomorrow, we'll be home in our own beds."

"I know." Except I don't know. Anything can happen out here. It's just as likely that we will never see our own beds again.

My helmet rolls against the cliff face. We've decided it's safer to keep the helmets on all night rather than risk being hit by more falling rock. Sitting up, it's impossible to find any kind of comfortable position. It feels like I have a bowling ball strapped to my head. Every time I shift, the sound of plastic crunching against rock fills my ears.

Far off in the valley, the eerie cry of coyotes rises into the cold air. I hug my knees to my chest. Shivering, I pull myself deeper into my puffy jacket, tug the hood up over my helmet and tighten the drawstrings. With my arms wrapped around my knees and my feet jammed up close to my backside, I don't take up much space.

I press my chin to my knees and concentrate on slowing my breathing.

The dreams begin almost before I am properly asleep. I jerk wildly, whirling my arms and legs as I fall through empty space, soaring down toward the jagged rocks waiting below. I half wake, touch my tether and pull my arms and legs back in close, trying to contain my pounding heart. Somehow I drift back into another dream. This time I am taping up Lissy's leg, and when I tug to make sure the tape is secure, her leg comes off in my hands. I stare down at the detached limb and scream, so startled I drop it over the edge. We all watch it tumble end over end until it disappears.

"Ayla?" Carlos's voice calls out to me. "Are you okay?"

"Thanks. It was just a dream."

Carlos's light clicks on, and he shines it on Andrei's face.

"He's still breathing," he says.

It's ridiculous how that sounds like amazingly good news. The light blinks out. Once again each of us is an island of cold and dark on the ledge, like birds stranded on a high tension wire. Lissy groans and mutters but does not wake up. She probably has the most comfortable perch of all of us, with her back against the corner at the far end of the ledge and her feet more or less straight out in front of her.

My knees quiver and my teeth chatter.

"I can hear you from over here," Carlos says. Then after a moment he adds, "Is there room beside you?"

I reach out and feel around the ledge. "A bit. Why?"

He doesn't answer, but I can hear him moving around—the clink of something at the anchor, his breathing, the rustle of his jacket. "Don't move," he says, flashing the light on.

He's standing, navigating his way carefully over and around Andrei. He has extended his leash a little so he can step over me. He crouches down beside me and then sits, his feet dangling over the ledge. He clicks the light off again, and I feel his arm across my shoulders. He wriggles a bit closer and pulls me in beside him. My teeth won't stop chattering. He rubs his hands up and down my arms, trying to warm me up.

"I'm so c-c-c-cold," I say and lean into him.

He wraps his other arm around me. "Lean against me," he says. "We'll both stay warmer."

He squeezes my cold fingers and we huddle together, awkward in our helmets and bulky coats. It's strange, snuggling with Carlos in the dark. He and Lissy have spent so much time together, almost from the first day we met him. Even though he and I are pressed close together now, it doesn't feel like anything more—or less—than survival.

"Carlos?"

"Hmm?"

"Why did you bring a can of spray paint with you?"

He doesn't answer right away. "When did you see that?"

"When we were going through the packs. Are you going to tag a rock or something?"

"Tagging is for people who can't paint," he says. Though he doesn't move his arm, I feel him stiffen.

There's another long silence as we sit side by side in the dark. I shouldn't have brought it up. It's none of my business what he chooses to do.

"I was going to paint a spider up at the top," he says. "This is going to sound weird."

He shifts beside me and pulls me a little closer. "I wanted to leave my mark on the mountain. I thought it would be cool to paint a spider at every summit I reach."

His explanation doesn't sound that weird. I don't agree with him, but it makes sense if you're someone like Carlos. He isn't finished.

"I'm not going to do it though."

At first I think it's because we didn't get to the top. But that's not it at all.

"It's like the mountain knows we're here," he says. "I don't want to piss her off."

In the dark, I turn toward him. I wish I could see the expression on his face.

"I know," he says. "Crazy, hey?"

A gust of wind blows across the ledge, and I shiver. I squeeze his hand in mine. "No," I say. "Not crazy at all."

He gives me a little hug, and I lean against him. To my surprise I drift off again and don't wake up until the sound of retching tears me out of my uneasy sleep.

# Chapter Nineteen

"Andrei?"

"Dad?"

The sounds Andrei makes are right out of a horror movie. He is heaving and choking, coughing and spitting.

"He's puking all over the ledge," Carlos says, scrambling to his feet. He makes his way back along the ledge until he's at Andrei's head. Andrei is confused and trying to sit up, wiping at the back of his mouth with his hand.

"Where am I?" he asks. "What happened?" Then he groans and retches again. He must already have puked up whatever little bit of food was left in him because all that comes out is a bit of yellow spit. I have to look away.

"Dad! You can hear us?"

Andrei slumps sideways again and only manages a groan for an answer. He coughs, tries again to sit up and looks around. "Where am I?" he repeats. "What happened?"

"A rock hit you. You've been unconscious all night. How do you feel now?" Carlos asks.

"Where am I?" Andrei answers. "What happened?" He lies back down and closes his eyes.

"A rock hit you on the head. You're above Black Dog Falls. Remember?"

Andrei responds with deep breathing.

"Andrei?" I say. "Are you awake?"

"Dad! Wake up! We need you!" There's an edge of desperation to Lissy's voice that is almost scarier than the empty space looming beneath us. The sun is coming up, and the sharp teeth of the rocks below are becoming visible again.

"Should we wait a bit? In case he comes to?" Carlos asks.

Lissy nods. "Maybe. Maybe he'll wake up enough that you can help him down. And if somehow you can lower me..."

It sounds like a questionable plan to me, but I don't say anything.

"It would be better to all go together," Carlos says. That much I agree with, but as the sky lightens I can't see how we could carry Lissy and deal with Andrei if he is going to keep passing out.

"Why don't we pick a time?" I suggest. "Say, 9:00 am. While we're waiting, we can pack what we would need to take so we are ready to go. Lissy, you have to explain exactly how we need to set up the ropes to rappel. If Andrei is awake by nine, we can go together. If not, we're back to our original plan."

Carlos and Lissy nod. "Okay," Carlos says. "That also gives us a chance to have some breakfast. Lissy?"

"Fine," Lissy says. "I'll make something. Except—" A pained look creases her forehead. "Except I really have to pee, and I can't exactly squat."

Carlos turns bright pink.

"Why are *you* embarrassed?" Lissy asks. "I'm the one who has to pee. Ayla, you'll have to help me."

"How?"

"I'd pee in my pants except then I'd be sitting here in wet clothes for however long it takes us to get out of here. That's a fast ticket to hypothermia land."

She has a point. Carlos lets out a little more slack in my tether so I can sidestep along the ledge and crouch down beside Lissy. "I'll kind of roll over onto my side with my butt pointed that way," she says, jabbing her chin in the direction of the edge. "Can you undo my harness leg straps? Then you'll have to pull my pants down and hold me steady. I should be able to aim so it dribbles away from me."

"I can't believe we're having this conversation," I say.

"That makes two of us." She rolls her hips to the side and holds on to me, being careful to move her leg as little as possible. "The splint is working great," she says grimly, her taut jaw telling me otherwise.

I tug at her pants, and she gasps in pain. "Sorry!"

"Keep going."

Behind us, Andrei starts retching again. I glance over my shoulder and see Carlos bent over him. "Where am I? What happened?"

"You were hit on the head by a rock," Carlos repeats patiently.

"Are you going to pee?" I ask when Lissy is in position.

"I'm trying," she says. "Now I can't—but I really have to go!"

"What happened?" Andrei says again. "Where are we?"

"Oh, I need to go so bad," Lissy moans.

I touch her shoulder and say, "Relax. Think of waterfalls. Rain running through gutters."

"Do you need a drink of water over there?" Carlos asks, politely not looking up.

Under my hand, Lissy's shoulders start to quiver. At first I think she's crying or shivering—or both. Then I realize she is laughing, a desperate, silent laugh. Tears squeeze out of the corners of her eyes. "This is so not funny," I say, averting my eyes from my friend's bare backside.

Then she is laughing so hard she has no choice but to let go. In a moment, she is done. We pull her pants back up, still giggling, fasten her leg straps and get her settled back into her place at the end of the shelf.

"You guys had better be fast," she says. "I don't think I can manage to do that on my own."

That's when I know we won't be trying to take Andrei and Lissy with us. Carlos and I are going to have to descend on our own. Lissy divides up our breakfast portions and starts talking about anchors and rappelling. I've been trying not to think about what's ahead of us when we descend. It's almost enough to make my stomach tighten so much I can't eat, except I'm so hungry I'd happily chew off my right arm. I gobble down my share of a granola bar and a small handful of nuts and raisins.

Then, as Lissy patiently explains what we will have to do, Carlos and I take turns repeating back the instructions. If we make a mistake going down, we will die. It's not a joke. Not a paranoid statement made by a person who worries too much. That's the reality of our situation. More accidents happen when people rappel than during any other maneuver on a mountain. More accidents happen on descents than going up. More accidents happen to people who don't know what they are doing than to those with more experience. If I add up the factors that increase the likelihood of disaster, the chance of Carlos and I getting down in one piece is not great.

Andrei groans and tries to roll over. We all watch as he is stopped by the rope tied to his harness. "Where are we?" he says. "What happened?"

"Hey, how are you doing, Andrei?" Carlos sounds like he's just run into Andrei at the grocery store.

Andrei groans and coughs. "What happened? Where am I?"

"We're above Black Dog Falls. Remember?"

"How did we get here?"

At least it's a different question.

"Do you want a drink of water?" I ask.

"Oh yes, please. Where are we? What happened?"

I pass Carlos a water bottle. He kneels and holds the water bottle to Andrei's mouth. Andrei takes a drink, swallows and then groans again. "Is this water?"

Carlos and I look at each other. Is that really what Andrei wants to know?

"More?" Carlos asks.

Andrei reaches clumsily for the bottle at the same time Carlos extends his hand. We watch in horror as the hard plastic water bottle flies out of Carlos's hand and soars into the air. It sails a long way before it smashes against a rock and shatters.

"Dad!" Lissy's anger shocks me. Obviously, Andrei didn't mean to send the water bottle flying. A wave of guilt washes over me. How many times have I lost my patience with my dad since his accident?

"What happened?" Andrei asks again before closing his eyes and sinking back onto the ledge.

Dad was like that too. At first he couldn't remember anything. Couldn't string words together. He also hurt his back, which still bothers him. It's hard not to think about what else Andrei might have broken.

"We should get going," Carlos says. "We'll just have a drink before we go. There are empty containers back at camp. We'll be fine. It's not like we're hiking a thousand miles before we find water. We just have to get down to camp. It's not that far."

I force my mind back to what Carlos and I have to do next. Five steep pitches lie between us and safety. That's five times we need to figure out anchors and rappel down.

And if neither of us gets hurt, it's still a good hike to get back to the tents and even farther to get to a place where we can call for help.

"Lissy—will you be okay?"

She sucks in her bottom lip and looks past me, over the valley toward the edge of the lake and safety. "Carlos is right. It's just a broken leg. It's going to suck sitting up here, but it's not going to kill me."

With that, Carlos and I each take a pack and the essential items we will need to get down. I squat beside Lissy and give her a big hug. "We'll be back soon," I say. "Or, I mean, we'll send someone back who can get you out of here."

"I know," she says. She turns her head away, but not before I see the tears running over her cheeks.

"You'll be okay," I say. "And so will your dad."

# Chapter Twenty

The first anchor takes so long to get organized, I think we won't ever leave the ledge.
Lissy fires a string of instructions at Carlos
and me.

"Thread one end of the rope through
the ring at the end of the anchor chain.
Yep—and now through the second chain."

Once I've poked the end of the rope
through the rings on both chains, I keep
pulling.

"No. Stop—don't pull it all the way through. It won't be long enough. Tie the end of the second rope to the first one."

"Oh. Right."

"An overhand knot is fine. Carlos, make sure you have knots at the other end of each rope. You don't want to rappel off the ends of your ropes."

Yuck. I feel ill. Carlos and I try to follow her instructions and set up practice rappels with our belay devices. I am surprised he hasn't had more experience doing this. Then again, if you climb without ropes you find other ways to get down. Like the fire escape down to the alley behind the Liberty Theater.

"Now you have to back up your rappel with a Prusik." Lissy tries to describe how to wrap a piece of cord around the ropes to make a kind of emergency friction brake.

"Like this?"

"No, you have to start by clipping one end to your leg loop."

I fumble with the knot. My fingers are cold and refuse to work properly.

"And now wrap the cord—and again..."

Carlos tries to follow the instructions, but his luck is no better.

"No! Not like that! You have to clip the other end back too—"

"Back where?" I am about ready to throttle her or give up, except we don't have a choice—if we don't set up properly, we will smash ourselves just like that water bottle.

"Can you show me what you mean?" I ask, already edging along the shelf.

She takes the thin cord and wraps it around and around the ropes I'll be lowering myself on. "Clip it like this. Below but not too close to the belay device or it will jam. Don't skip this step. That's your backup—in case a rock hits you or you panic," she says pointedly. But her hands are shaking, and she's gone quite pale. Maybe she's finally realizing it isn't a good idea to drag your useless, scared-of-mountains friends along on expeditions like this. Maybe now she won't be so keen to leave the gym. "Your turn."

I try to do what she did. But her fingers moved too fast, and somehow when I pull on the cord, it falls away from the ropes. That wouldn't hold much in an accident.

"Like this," she says and does it again, more slowly this time. "You had it right. You just missed your carabiner when you went to clip. You have to watch what you're doing."

Carlos also follows along. He manages to figure it out just before I do.

"Okay," Lissy says. "Just remember to check the system before you lean back and lower yourselves. Check each other. Then check your own setup again. Okay?"

"Okay. Ready, Carlos?"

"Ready when you are."

We move back over toward the anchor. "Ladies first," Carlos says.

"Now is not the time to be polite," I say. There is no way I'm going to be the first to lower myself into the abyss. "You go first. You're a better climber."

"That doesn't mean—"

"Stop arguing," Lissy says. "Carlos, you should go first."

His tongue flicks out over his bottom lip. Wow. He's nervous. Realizing this doesn't exactly fill me with confidence.

"Fine. I've got this," he says, finishing his setup. "See you down there." He turns his head and looks down before stepping backward off the ledge. A few minutes later he yells, "Secure!"

Once he's down and there's some slack in the ropes, I get myself set up. I hold on to the sling at the anchor with one hand and clutch my brake hand tightly around the twinned ropes running out the bottom of my belay device. The Prusik knot swirls around and around and connects to my leg loop. If I let go for any reason, that little piece of cord is going to save me. It looks about as strong as a piece of thread. Despite the slug of water I just took, I am parched. My lips are dry and chapped from the cold night outside.

"Lean back," Lissy says. "Check the system."

I lean back without letting go. The ropes tighten. They are threaded through my belay device and through the rings at the anchor. Everything looks good.

"You're good to go," Lissy says. "Relax. You need to unclip your sling and take it with you. You'll need it for the next anchor." I do as she says and ease backward, my legs shaking. Any moment now I'm going to puke up my tiny bit of breakfast. I undo the carabiner from the anchor and secure the sling to a gear loop on the side of my harness. Even this simple action is awkward because I can only use one hand. Hanging backward off the edge of the ledge, all my weight is now on the rappel system.

"Go," Lissy says. "Clip in when you get to the next station, and thread the next rappel anchor with Carlos. Just like you did for this one. Okay?"

No words form in my dry mouth.

"Don't forget which rope to pull on—the blue, not the green. Or the knot will jam in the anchor."

There's no way I'm going to remember everything she has said. All I can do is dumbly start walking backward down the face of the cliff, descending into space. My heart thuds, and I concentrate on moving my hands smoothly. I ease the rope through the belay device, careful not to tangle or foul the safety knot. Down. Down. Down. One short bit of rope let out after another. And finally my feet touch the next ledge.

"Hey, Carlos."

"Hey, Ayla. Good job."

With one hand clamped around the brake ends of the ropes, I fish around for the locking carabiner on my gear loop. *Snap.* It clicks into place. I check that the sling is still looped through it, rotate the lock and double-check to make sure everything is closed and secured. For the fiftieth time, I check that the other end of the sling is still hitched to my harness. I stand up and move closer to the anchor. Ease off the tension on the rappel rope.

The loose ends of the ropes hanging down just beyond the ledge are still knotted.

"One down. Four to go," Carlos says.

"Which one do we pull?" I ask.

"What do you mean?" Carlos says,

starting to pull on the green rope. "What difference does it make?"

"Stop! The rope could jam up there!"

"Oh. Right." We both stare at the two ropes. What did Lissy say?

"It's the blue one. Take the knot out of the end."

Carlos starts to pull. I half expect I've got it wrong, but the ropes pull smoothly.

It takes longer to get organized for lowering ourselves off the next ledge. Without Lissy there to guide us, we second-guess everything we do. Finally, Carlos is set up to rappel. I check everything over before he leans back and tests the system. "Looks good," I say.

Carlos is still secured to the anchor with his sling and carabiner. He throws first one rope and then the other over the edge. When they snap tight, he jumps a little and then laughs. "Heavy suckers," he says. Then he smiles. "You're doing great," he says. "We're going to be fine."

With that he unfastens his sling from the anchor, leans backward and steps away from the safety of the ledge.

# Chapter Twenty-One

The next two pitches go smoothly enough. We get into a rhythm and a routine, keeping everything tidy and well organized when we reach each anchor. At the top of the fourth and final pitch, I start pulling on the blue rope. Carlos snakes a neat stack back and forth over his sling.

I've only just settled into a good rhythm of hand-over-hand pulling when the rope gets caught. I give it a good tug, but nothing moves.

"Are you pulling on the right rope?"

"I think so." I give it another yank.

"It must be stuck," Carlos says.

"I think it's the big knot. It must be jammed somewhere. I can't see exactly."

The knot tying our two ropes together is bulky. This isn't the first time it has snagged, but we've always been able to jiggle it loose.

"Let me try." Carlos flips the rope as hard as he can. It slaps against the rock, but the knot does not pop free. He flicks it this way and that and gives a couple of really hard yanks. No luck. The rope is stuck fast.

"Now what?" The length of rope we've pulled so far isn't even long enough to reach halfway down the last pitch.

"I can climb up and free the knot," Carlos says.

"It's way up there. We can't risk another injury, so don't even think about going up unprotected."

"We don't have any gear," he points out.

True enough. We wanted to move fast and keep our load light. Besides, rappelling shouldn't require any fancy equipment.

He reaches behind him for the few bits and pieces hanging from his gear loops. "What do we have?" Lissy had insisted we each take some quickdraws and slings. We unclip everything we have. Six draws, four spare carabiners and five slings—two long and three short.

"You'll need to stay attached to the anchor with a locker and a sling," Carlos says, "while you belay me."

Good. At least he isn't going to do anything crazy.

"I can use that tree..."

About a dozen feet above us, a scraggly tree grows out of the rock at a strange angle.

"And above that it looks like maybe I could put a sling around something where those rocks are sticking out?"

"We don't have much choice," I say and start to set up the belay while he ties into the end of the rope. "Good luck."

"Climbing."

Carlos climbs carefully and makes it to the tree without incident. He gives the tree a shake. "Seems solid enough." With the sling looped around the trunk and the draw clipped into the ends, he is able to secure the rope. Only when I hear the click of the carabiner gate do I let out my breath.

"There isn't much to work with," he says, moving up the face. Nervously I feed out the rope, calculating how far he has traveled, how much slack is in the system, how far he has moved past the safety of his tree protection.

"Don't go too much farther," I call up. If he comes off now, he will take quite a fall. He'll probably hit the ledge I'm standing on.

"There's nowhere good to put a sling," he says.

I try to stay calm, to not think about what will happen if he falls. He's struggling to get around the same overhang that gave us trouble yesterday. He strains and grunts and jams his foot into a corner. Not expecting to climb, we're both wearing our approach shoes. He doesn't have the same kind of traction he did in his rock-climbing shoes.

*Please. Don't. Fall.* I know this kind of thinking is useless, but as Carlos struggles to get up and around the lump of rock, I mutter the plea a dozen times. My hands ache from clamping the rope so tightly.

And then he's over the obstacle and in a secure-enough spot to fasten two slings together and loop them around a rock. He snaps a draw to the slings and the rope to the draw. I swallow hard.

"I can see it! Not far above me. The knot is jammed into a crack behind another rock."

He's climbing again, more quickly now, and I have to pay attention to keep the rope feeding out smoothly.

"That wasn't going anywhere!" he calls down. "Can you give me some slack? I'll make a rappel anchor here with the last sling."

"Okay."

After a few minutes he yells, "Rope!" and the loose rope slithers down, mostly landing on the ledge. Carlos rappels back down to the double slings above the jutting rock and takes them apart. He climbs back down until he's level with the tree and retrieves the gear from there too. Then he's back at my side and clipping into the anchor.

"Good job," I say. "Thanks for going up."

"You know what I was thinking about up there?"

"How much better it is to have a top rope?"

His hands shake a little as he sorts out the ropes and gets ready to set up our final rappel.

"Almost. I was thinking about the time Alain Robert—that French guy who climbs buildings? How one time he had a panic attack halfway up a climb and had to be rescued."

"Really?"

"I was scared. I thought I wasn't going to get around that rock."

I look up at the tricky spot. Yep. If he had fallen there, we would have been in big trouble.

I put my hand on his shoulder. "You did great. We're almost down."

# Chapter Twenty-Two

The final pitch is easy. When my feet touch down, I burst into tears. Carlos puts his arms around me and pulls me close. It's only then that I realize he is crying too. And this makes me stop as if someone has thrown a bucket of icy-cold water over my head. We are alive. We are down. We are going to be okay.

"Hey," I say, pulling back a little and touching his cheek.

He straightens up and wipes the back of his hand across his face.

"Let's go find some water. I'm so thirsty I can hardly stand it," he says. "Should we risk drinking some of this or wait until we're back at camp?"

We both look longingly at the water-fall cascading down over the rocks. I'm desperately thirsty, so its gurgling and chortling seems like mockery.

"I think the last thing we need to do is get sick from drinking untreated water," I say. "I hear the cramps are awful."

He grins like he had never worried about anything. "You're right. We're, what, two hours away at most?"

I nod. Two hours seems like forever. "I can get that far. Not a step more though."

We pull the ropes for the very last time. Some lucky climber will find a sling and a draw partway up, where Carlos set up the emergency rappel anchor. We leave the ax and other trail-clearing tools behind too.

"Let's go," Carlos says. And just like that we are moving again, hurrying along the narrow path, heading back toward camp.

It must have taken us longer than we'd thought to rappel off the mountain and free the stupid rope. It is already well into the afternoon by the time we reach the campsite.

"Poor Lissy," I say. "She must be desperate up there." Even though I know it's no use, I check for a cell signal. Nothing.

We don't even bother pumping and purifying water. Instead we add purification tablets to water straight from the lake. It will take a little time for the water to be safe, so in the meantime we open two tins of peaches and slurp them down. Then we set off again, moving as fast as we can though we are both tired. The daylight lasts until we're about halfway to the parking lot. Under the trees, it's darker than out in the open, and we have to switch on the headlamp. We only have one between us, so one of us is always struggling to see.

Even though we try to push on and move quickly, it's slow going. It's impossible to see where we are or how far we've come. We can't see beyond the circle of white light. My eyes try to adjust, but the minute I look away, blackness takes over everything.

We take turns going in front. When it's my turn to lead, I move the light so I can see the trail ahead and then shine it behind so Carlos can see. It's when I am trying to negotiate a sharp turn on a steeper section of trail that I hear Carlos take a hard fall behind me.

"Carlos? Are you okay?"

He answers with a string of swearwords.

"What did you do?"

"My ankle. I twisted it. I'll be okay. Just give me a minute."

I squat beside him and shine the light on his foot. He's holding on to it, his face contorted with pain.

"Is it broken?" I ask. This can't be happening.

"I don't think so. Help me up."

I hold his arm, and he lurches to his good leg. When he tries to put weight on the hurt foot, he gasps and lifts it off the ground. "Maybe I can hop if you help me."

We move about twenty feet down the trail, Carlos leaning heavily on me. It's awkward, not just because he's quite a bit heavier than I am, but also because the trail is narrow and uneven. It's nearly impossible to stay beside him.

"This isn't going to work," I say.

"I know," he agrees. "You'll be much faster without me. I'll be fine. Keep the light on—you should have enough battery."

I don't want to leave him, but we don't have a choice. "Are you sure you'll be okay? I'll bring back help as soon as I can."

"I'll be fine. If you aren't back by dawn, I'll start hopping down the trail."

"It's probably better if you stay put. You don't need to fall again."

I help him get settled under a tree at the side of the trail. "Will you be warm enough?" I wish we had brought more clothes with us. We should have taken more time at camp. Should have thought through what we might need. I pull the thin plastic rain poncho from the lid of my pack. "Here. Take this."

"I can't believe I'm going to wear that," he says.

"Who's going to see you out here?"

"Good point."

"Who gets the water?" he asks. We only have one bottle between us.

"You keep it. I'll take a good drink before I go. I'll be in civilization before you."

We split the small amount of food we threw into the pack while we were back in camp. "Don't eat it all at once," I joke.

"Good luck," he says.

I kneel beside him and give him a quick hug. "You'll be okay. I'll get back as fast as I can."


It's just after midnight when I leave Carlos at the side of the trail. On my own, I move faster than we were able to even before Carlos hurt his ankle. I keep the pool of light trained just ahead of my feet and don't let myself look to either side. If I do, I can see how steeply the embankment drops off at the side of the trail. The tumble down toward the creek probably wouldn't kill me, but the last thing I need at this point is yet another injury. The rescuers would have a hard time finding the bodies scattered all over the wilderness.

The trail twists and winds, loops around and through the trees, uphill and downhill. I keep going, thankful I'm not carrying out the same amount of weight I had when we hiked in. In the dark, even with the light, my progress is slow. It's hard to tell the difference between a shadow, a puddle and a rock. Several times I stumble, and once I trip over a branch and crash down hard enough to bring tears to my eyes. I kneel in the dark, my hands on the wet, muddy ground beside me. "Get up," I tell myself sternly. "Keep going."

I am just beginning to wonder if I've somehow missed the parking lot when the trees open up and the rough trail spits me out onto the gravel. The windows and reflectors glint back at me when I point the light in the car's direction. I pull out my phone and check for a signal. *Yes.*

I start to dial 9-1-1. Before the call goes through, the screen goes black. *What?*

No amount of shaking, button pressing or swearing makes the screen light up again. The battery must be dead. *No!*

Now what?

I try to open the car, but it is securely locked. Why on earth didn't Carlos and I think to bring along the car keys? I don't have my license yet, but I could at least have driven as far as the highway. This is an emergency. I can't imagine what Lissy is thinking up there on the cliff. I wonder if Andrei is properly conscious. And what about Carlos? He's safe enough, but even with the rain poncho, he doesn't really have enough clothing to stay warm. And if it starts to rain again...

How far are we from the highway? I can't remember exactly how long the drive was, but it seems like it took quite some time after we turned off. I wonder about sprinting back to Carlos to—what? Give him my sweatshirt? Even though I've been moving steadily, I'm still chilled. It makes no sense to go back.

Andrei. Lissy. Carlos. They are all counting on me. There's nobody else left to go for help. I move off down the road, keeping the light pointed in front of me. Without the phone, I have no idea what time it is. I should have checked the time before I started to dial. How much longer before dawn? Will I get to the highway before first light?

# Chapter Twenty-Three

What is there to think about when you are dog-tired, hungry and thirsty, and slogging along a dark road? I think about my dad. How if he knew what was going on, he would be worried. And then I reconsider. Maybe if he knew what was going on—me plodding along one foot in front of the other—he wouldn't give it a second thought. Maybe it's *not* knowing that's actually scary. I mean, I am tired and my feet hurt and I am just about ready to get down on my knees and drink from a puddle. But I can't say that I'm scared. Fear would stop me right here. I would sit down, curl up in a ball and imagine all the terrible things that could happen to Lissy, to Andrei, to Carlos—to me. A cougar could leap down on me from the trees. I could wipe out and hit my head, and the first vehicle to trundle along the road would run me over.

But I'm not obsessing about any of these possibilities. Mostly I am thinking that if I can reach the next bend without stopping, I will be that much closer to getting help. And getting to the next bend is a manageable task. At the next bend, I shine the beam of my light ahead and pick out the shape of a tree. That becomes my next goal. The tree, then a big rock and then a dark patch on the gravel road—a puddle.

One landmark at a time, I force myself to keep going, even when the light dims, flickers and goes out. It's amazing how when your eyes have had a chance to adjust, you can see enough to keep moving. Especially when the moon is out and the cloud cover is light. I keep pushing onward, from one shadowy form to another, until I hear something that sounds like the rush of water. It's fading in and out, and then I realize it's actually the sound of car tires on pavement.

The highway! I move faster, and as I come around the last bend I see the road stretching away in either direction. Occasional headlights blaze across the asphalt. I reach the highway and wait for the next vehicle, then wave my arms wildly and watch the taillights zoom into the distance without stopping. "No! Stop!"

Two more vehicles fly past before a pickup truck slows and a woman pulls over.

"Honey! I thought you were a deer! What are you doing all the way out here?"

At the hospital the next day, Lissy sits in a wheelchair beside Andrei's bed. Her leg is in a cast, and several people have already scrawled greetings on it. "The helicopter was so loud!" Lissy says, her eyes widening.

"They lowered two rescue guys and then this stretcher thing."

"I wish I could have seen that," Carlos says from where he sits on a visitor's chair. His sprained ankle is propped up on the wastepaper basket. "A walking stick I made myself was all I had to help me. Well, and Ayla, of course."

When I had returned to the parking lot with the woman who had stopped to pick me up, Carlos was already waiting by the car. He had managed to get himself that far by using a sturdy branch as a walking stick and half hopping, half hobbling along the trail.

"I would have enjoyed the ride if my..." Andrei's voice trails off, and he lifts his hand to touch the side of his head.

"Your head?" Lissy prompts.

"Yes. My head hurt so much." Andrei still looks pale, sitting up in bed. Though he suffered a bad concussion, luckily he didn't have any kind of neck or back injury. He's having a bit of trouble keeping up with the conversation though. And he can't seem to find the right words when he tries to join in.

"I had to wait while they flew Dad out. Oh, the rescue guys said you did a great job with the splint."

"Ayla, how can we ever thank you enough?" We all turn as Lissy's mom comes into the room, her arms open wide.

Her arms wrap tightly around me in a big hug. She squeezes me until I can hardly breathe. When she lets go and steps back, her eyes are moist. "And you too, Carlos. Thank you both."

Carlos clears his throat and suddenly seems very interested in something outside the window. "You're welcome," he mumbles.

Lissy grins at Andrei and touches his hand. I remember my relief when they let me see my dad after his surgery. I thought everything would be fine because he was alive.

"The doctor says you can go home tomorrow," Lissy's mom is saying.

Andrei smiles. "I will be so happy to be sleeping in my own..." He falters and pats the pillow. "Yes. Home."

Andrei's not the only one who wants to go home. Yesterday my dad and I came straight to the hospital to wait for Andrei and Lissy to be brought in by the helicopter. When I finally got home, I collapsed into bed. I can't remember ever sleeping so soundly or for so long. What finally shook me out of my deep sleep this morning was the smell of pancakes! It's been a long time since Dad made breakfast for us. This morning, on the way back to the hospital, he said quietly, his voice shaking a little, *That could have been you.*

Now, in Andrei's room, I catch Dad watching me. What's he thinking? I smile, and he swallows hard and turns away. A familiar sinking feeling settles in my stomach. He has turned away so many times since his accident. But this time, he turns and looks back at me. He winks, and his face brightens with a huge grin. I don't know how this happened, these changes, the healing, but they are so obvious now. I guess they've been going on while I was concentrating on what's still wrong. What he can't or won't do. But he is here. And he is smiling.

On Thursday after school, all three of us meet back in the climbing gym. Lissy and Carlos have matching sets of crutches and aren't climbing anything. I clip into the auto-belay and dip my fingers into my chalk bag. As I start to climb, they offer feedback.

"I heard that clunky foot!" Lissy says when my toe bumps the wall.

"You should come down and do that again," Carlos says.

The route of blue holds stretches out in a wobbly line above me. I move to the left and place my right hand flat against the wall. Then I move my right foot to a small hold up to the right.

"Nice move," Carlos says.

"Not bad," Lissy agrees.

My back is to my friends, so they can't see me smiling.

"I was thinking," Lissy says, "that we should plan a backpacking trip for the spring. Maybe up through Springdale Meadows?"

Carlos pulls out his notebook. "My birthday is at the end of August, and I still need eighteen summits."

"Yeah, that didn't work out too well, hey? If we go up for a week, like during spring break, maybe we could do some ice climbing."

"Frozen waterfalls?" Carlos asks.

"Sure, on the way to the top. It's a perfect place for collecting summits. The peaks aren't actually that high. I mean, it will depend on the snow pack and avalanche conditions and—"

I keep climbing, one foot and then the other. I shift my weight and reach for the next hold.

They will ask if I want to come along. And though my stomach clenches at the thought, I will say yes. Because even though the nervousness is real, there's another sensation too. A kind of excitement about all the things I haven't experienced yet. Adventures I can't even imagine.

Three-quarters of the way up, I plant my feet and shake out first one arm and then the other. Down below, Lissy and Carlos are still chattering away. Missing out on whatever awaits them would be far worse than facing any challenges we might encounter up in the mountains.

"When's spring break?" I call down.

Lissy pulls out her phone to check, and I start to climb again. I keep going all the way to the top. I ring the brass bell, then kick back, let go and float back down to join my friends and make some plans.

# Acknowledgments

This book would not have been possible without the support and encouragement of dozens of members of the climbing community. To all of you who have patiently provided good beta and reliable belays, fine conversation and endless encouragement, your willingness to take in an ancient newbie has been one of the most positive experiences of my life. I won't even attempt to name you individually, because it would be impossible to do so without forgetting someone! It would be wrong, though, not to mention Fabio Lacentra's contributions as mentor, coach, butt kicker, friend, belayer, partner and technical climbing consultant for this novel. Fabio, *Deadpoint* really wouldn't have been the same book without your good-natured assistance.

Based on Vancouver Island, British Columbia, Nikki Tate spends as much time traveling as she does at home. The author of more than thirty books, Nikki loves the fact that she can take her laptop with her when she's off exploring the world and looking for cool places to climb.

Titles in the Series

# orca sports

# orca sports

For more information on all the books
in the Orca Sports series, please visit
**www.orcabook.com**.